Players in the Drama at Dower House

THE FAMILY

Anthony Funicelli   He has problems money can't cure.

Mama Rosa   Anthony's mother, a matriarch who'd stop at nothing if it would help her family.

Lucia   Anthony's luscious hand-picked wife. She is breeding an heir.

Hansel and Gretchen   Anthony's rebellious offspring from his first marriage.

Fredo Clemenza   A poor relation, who—too bad for him—is almost Anthony's double.

THE SERVANTS

Tip   The houseman, whose heavy indebtedness to Anthony is almost too heavy to bear.

Mrs. Flower   The cook. Some call her Mrs. Dour.

Jacob   Mrs. Flower's stern, violent son.

Noah   Jacob's gentle brother, who understands nothing of the evil around him.

Also by E. X. Giroux
Published by Ballantine Books:

A DEATH FOR A DARLING
A DEATH FOR A DIETITIAN
A DEATH FOR A DILETTANTE
A DEATH FOR A DOCTOR
A DEATH FOR A DREAMER
A DEATH FOR ADONIS
A DEATH FOR A DANCER

A DEATH FOR
A DOUBLE

E.X. Giroux

BALLANTINE BOOKS • NEW YORK

Library of Congress Catalog Card Number: 89-24108

ISBN 0-345-36833-9

This edition published by arrangement with St. Martin's Press, Inc.

Manufactured in the United States of America

First Ballantine Books Edition: August 1991

This book is for
Jessie and John Brock,
who have the Gold
and are reaching
for the Diamond

A DEATH
FOR A
DOUBLE

CHAPTER ONE

Robert Forsythe decided he might qualify for the *Guinness Book of World Records* as the only person in London who had never entered any of the outlets of a world-famous chain of hamburger restaurants. If that was the case, he was about to ruin his own record. He cast a look at the garish tubes of golden light that flanked the entrance, a door hissed automatically and hospitably open, and he stepped into the restaurant.

The immediate impression was that the place had originally been a warehouse. It was the right size and the ceiling soared far above his head, but there the resemblance ceased. Generally, warehouses were poorly lit and tended to be dusty and grubby. This bright place fairly shrieked cleanliness. In fact, it looked as though it was thoroughly hosed out daily. Jets of water couldn't possibly damage the decor, which consisted of plastic materials and chrome. The serving counter that ran the length of the huge room, the dozens of round tables and modular chairs, even the baskets of brightly colored plants that hung from the beams were obviously constructed of plastic materials.

Spaced behind the counter was a row of servers ranging from teenagers to gray-haired oldsters, all uniformed in bright jackets and jaunty caps. Behind them, covering the wall, were menus in huge letters, no doubt also made of plastic.

The door behind Forsythe swished open and a couple of young men dressed in leather jackets and jeans stampeded in as though in the final throes of starvation. The taller lad thudded into Forsythe and, with no word of apology or even a sideways glance, bolted toward the counter. Stepping away from the door, Forsythe wondered whether to seek refuge at a table or await his host where he was. He decided to stand his ground. Sandy's favorite nephew might have difficulty locating him in the midst of that mob of eager eaters.

He put in his time looking the patrons over. The clientele ranged from babes in arms to senior citizens. Dress varied, but leather and denim appeared to predominate, and although there was a merciful absence of piped-in music, the sound level was appalling. Long lines of patrons snaked up to each of the attendants behind the counter, but the service was rapid. Trays piled with boxes and small cartons were thrust into waiting hands, money was exchanged, and patrons hurried to take tables. To Forsythe's left, in a fenced enclosure, about a dozen small children were ranged around a table presided over by a couple of harried-looking matrons. Most of the tots were wearing paper hats, blowing on paper horns, whirling noisemakers, and looking delighted. The exception was one little chap howling his lungs out and furiously throwing chips at the plumper matron. Around the table cavorted a chap dressed as a clown and a shorter one disguised as a plastic hamburger.

Happy birthday, Forsythe thought wearily, and wondered where in hell Buford Sanderson was. Let's get this over with, he urged silently, so I can get out of this madhouse. A hand touched his arm and he turned.

"Sorry to be late," the young man at his elbow apologized. "Have you been waiting long?"

"Just arrived. Good to see you, Buffy," Forsythe said.

"After I rang you up, I had second thoughts and nearly called back to arrange to meet you somewhere a little more—" Buffy's eyes swept over Forsythe's sober dark suit and overcoat "—a bit more quiet. But to be frank, this is about all I can afford right now. Exchequer a bit strained, you know."

Forsythe laughed. "How well I remember. When I was an undergraduate, the exchequer was always strained. This place is fine." He pointed at the counter. "Shall we queue up?"

"You grab a table and I'll get the chow. Anything you fancy?"

"A hamburger and chips would be great."

"You came to the right place for that." Buffy added expansively, "I'll get Super Doopers. Pick a quiet table."

Now that may be a bit difficult, to say nothing of impossible, Forsythe decided as he wended his way among tables, trying to put as much distance as he could between the riotous birthday party and the seats he selected. As he sat down, a girl at the next table, clad entirely in black leather, glanced over, grinned, and nudged her male companion. The boy didn't grin. As his eyes slid disdainfully over Forsythe, he snorted and turned back to his food. What do you expect the working uniform of a barrister to be? Forsythe asked silently. He hadn't had time to return to his flat and change, but had come directly from court. Even in this permissive era, jeans and sweat shirts wouldn't go over well in those august surroundings. In fact, he had never owned either of these items and he made a mental note that he simply must buy some.

Ignoring the young couple, he watched Buffy Sanderson take a place at the end of a queue. The lad blended in perfectly: shabby jeans, a washed-out blue sweat shirt, a denim jacket. He was a big chap with the build of a footballer and he had a mass of unruly light brown hair that was long enough not to be fashionable but looked as though he couldn't afford a haircut. No doubt the boy didn't have much pocket money. He'd entered Oxford on a scholarship and, as Sandy often mentioned, his father had followed family tradition and taken a post as a small-town vicar, with a great many children and a miserable income. When she had mentioned her brother Douglas, there had been a bitter note in Abigail Sanderson's voice and Forsythe could guess why. Douglas's and her father had been so hard pressed financially that he'd been eager to have a childless sister adopt his little Abigail and raise her. No doubt the child had been better educated and materially endowed than if her aunt Rose hadn't volunteered, but Forsythe knew Sandy felt as though she'd been exiled from her numerous brothers and sisters.

As he thought of his secretary, he wondered wistfully when she would be able to return to chambers. Perhaps it is true that no one is indispensable, but, for him, Sandy was. Not only did she keep things running smoothly in chambers but she was the only mother he ever had known. His own mother had died young and he'd been just a toddler when Abigail Sanderson, then his father's secretary, had assumed maternal duties.

Forsythe's thoughts were interrupted. A tray slid onto the table and Buffy doled out Styrofoam boxes. "Your gourmet dinner, Mr. Forsythe. A hamburger, chips, a chocolate milk shake."

The barrister glanced at the tray. "Salt?"

Buffy handed tiny envelopes over. "All the condiments, including vinegar and tomato sauce."

"Everything disposable. Doesn't this increase the overhead?"

"The reverse. When we're finished, we simply chuck all these wrappings in one of those rubbish bins. Table is cleared and no need for hired help to whip around cleaning up." Buffy worked a straw into his milk-shake container. "It was good of you to give Aunt Abigail leave to look after the house and the kids, Mr. Forsythe."

"I've repeatedly asked you to call me Robert."

"I know." Buffy shook his head. "Doesn't sound right."

"I'm not exactly Methuselah."

"I know that, too. You're what . . . about fifteen years my senior?"

"Not even that. However, if you prefer mister, so be it." Forsythe changed the subject. "How is your mother coming along?"

"Making a rather slow recovery. Mother was a bit rundown anyway and then that operation . . . but she'll be fine as long as she gets enough rest."

"How is Sandy making out with the children? How many are there? Seven?"

4

"Counting me, nine. Aunt Abigail has eight to look after, from seventeen to four. Most of them are easy to handle, but Paul and Peter, seven and six respectively, are holy terrors. They make Attila the Hun look mild. Aunt Abigail has them whipped into shape, though. Odd, she doesn't even raise her voice and the little devils positively quail."

Forsythe sprinkled salt over a paper cone of chips. "Sandy doesn't have to raise her voice. A case of the velvet tongue and the wooden spoon."

"She raised you, didn't she?"

"That she did."

Buffy glanced across the table. "How's the hamburger?"

"Better than I expected. In fact, rather tasty."

"We were lucky. They were making them up fresh. When business is less booming, you can get one that's been sitting under those heat lamps until I swear it's old enough to vote." The boy took the last bite of his burger and sat back, wiping his mouth with a paper napkin. He pulled out a crumpled pack of cigarettes. "Care for one?"

"No thanks. I seldom indulge. Except for my pipe, of course." Forsythe took out his pipe and tobacco pouch. "I'm surprised a medical student smokes. All the dire warnings about tobacco, you know."

The younger man grinned. "I seldom indulge myself. Only have an occasional cigarette. Usually when I'm nervous."

"You're nervous now?"

"Shaking in my boots."

The lad showed no signs of nervousness. The big hand lighting the cigarette was steady as a rock. The boy had a resemblance to his Aunt Abigail. The bone structure in his long face was similar, the firm mouth, long nose, the cool blue eyes. Perhaps that resemblance explained Forsythe's fondness for Buffy Sanderson. He'd better find out what the boy's problem was. "Do you need legal advice, Buffy?"

"If I did, you'd be the first one I'd ask. After all, according to reports, you're the foremost barrister in London. No, this difficulty requires what Aunt Abigail calls your hobby."

Forsythe laughed. "I'm not a private investigator."

"I'm well aware of that, but you have done some amazing

work in the detection field. And Aunt Abigail says you're hooked on crime stuff.''

"The pot calling the kettle black," Forsythe muttered. "Your aunt is just as hooked as I am but she refuses to admit it. However, let's stop fencing. What is your trouble?"

Buffy flicked ash into his hamburger box. "Not mine. I was talking to Aunt Abigail about this and she suggested . . . no, she insisted I speak with you. I told her I couldn't bother a man as busy as you and she said bosh, everything is slow in your chambers at present and you'd be interested."

"If you'd get to the point, I might be."

"Right. Now, to be concise. I have this friend . . . no, I'd better fill in the background. I don't suppose you remember the year I went to the States as an exchange student, do you?"

"As a matter of fact, yes. Sandy told me about it. Chicago, wasn't it? A wealthy American family. You were about fifteen."

"Sixteen. And so excited I could hardly sleep for nights before I left. At the last moment, my father got an overseas call from Anthony Funicelli. He's the father of the boy and girl who were to stay with my parents. Anthony said that his children had decided they wouldn't come; they wanted to go to their ranch in California instead. Anthony said that didn't matter; he wanted me to make the trip and stay with his family, anyway. He said, regardless of his twin brats, he'd given his word and that he always kept it. So—"

"How old is Anthony Funicelli?" Forsythe asked.

Buffy's brow furrowed. "He must be in his early fifties now, so he'd have been about forty-five then."

"You seem to have no difficulty calling him by his given name."

"That's what he insisted on from the first, when he met the plane at O'Hare. 'Call me Anthony,' he said, and I always have. It doesn't jar, either. Anthony's such a warm sort of person and he seems so young. Even then, he seemed about my age. And he made a wonderful host. Took me everywhere, to all sorts of things, ball games and zoos and restaurants. His mother, Mama Rosa, was good to me too, but her idea of entertainment is Culture with a capital *C:*

6

opera, ballet, museums. I must admit I preferred Anthony's company, and when I had to come home, I really missed him. He's kept in touch through the years. Sent cards and presents at Christmas and on my birthdays. He always said we'd meet again, and we have. About two weeks ago, I had a phone call from him. To my surprise, I found he's living in England now. When we met, he was a widower, but about a year ago he remarried. His wife is a pretty Italian girl who lived in the same village Anthony's grandfather and Mama Rosa came from, and she was educated in a convent.''

Buffy paused to snub his cigarette out. He promptly lit another and then he continued. ''Anthony explained that because of his young wife's cloistered background, he decided instead of taking her directly to Chicago, he'd buy a house in a quiet area of England and live there for a time. Sort of a halfway house, he called it. He has business interests in this country and the Continent so it worked out well and—''

Forsythe broke into the stream of words. ''What business is Funicelli in?''

The boy smiled widely. ''About any type you can mention. His grandfather started a chain of butcher shops in Chicago, his father expanded into a meat-packing concern, and Anthony, when his turn came, bought into electronics, computers, fast-food chains, airlines, and so on. The Funicellis are fabulously wealthy, and yet to meet Anthony, you'd never know it. He's so warm and kind and as common as—''

''Dirt?'' the barrister suggested dryly.

Buffy's smile widened and became a laugh. ''I do tend to rave on, don't I? To try and shorten this, Anthony invited me down to visit and I got back yesterday. I spoke to Aunt Abigail and, as I mentioned, she suggested I ring you up—''

''It's obvious the problem is Anthony Funicelli's. Would you explain?''

''This is where it gets tough and why I'm nervous. It's all so . . . so nebulous. When I arrived at the Dower House, Anthony's home, everything seemed rather wonderful. Mama Rosa is there and his wife, of course, and she's pregnant. His twin children are visiting, too. At first, Anthony seemed much as I remembered him. Then I noticed he seemed rather

7

abstracted and jumpy. He kept asking me questions about you and Aunt Abigail. Seems he's read about your cases and he wondered if you were as much like Sherlock Holmes as it sounded or if the reporters had simply built you up. I told him you'd taken over on some crimes the police had virtually given up on and that you'd solved them. Then he said he'd like to meet both of you and wondered if you'd consent to visit him and his family for a few days. I explained that Aunt Abigail had her hands full with the vicarage and a horde of kids, and then he hinted maybe I could speak to you." Buffy spread both hands. "That's about it."

Forsythe looked into the pale blue eyes. "Better tell me the rest."

A tide of warm color swept up the young face. "What do you mean?"

"So far, all I know is that Funicelli was 'abstracted and jumpy.' He was curious about Sandy and me. Any man in his position must have business worries. His interest in me . . . possibly simple curiosity. There has to be something else."

"There is, but it sounds so . . ." Buffy's eyes dropped and he started gathering up the debris and piling it on the tray. "Anthony was in his office and I wanted to speak to him, so I ran up the stairs and flung open the door. I suppose I should have knocked but I didn't bother. It's such an informal household. Anthony was seated at his desk and when I went lunging in, he pulled open a drawer and put his hand in it. When he realized it was me, he pushed the drawer shut in a hurry, but I'd seen what he'd been reaching for. There was a revolver in that drawer. Mr. Forsythe, Anthony acted as though he was terrified."

The barrister checked his pipe, found it was out, and stuck it in his pocket. He said slowly, "A man in his position can afford the best of professional help. If he doesn't want the police, there are numerous agencies with first-rate private investigators. I can understand your concern but—"

"Please, Mr. Forsythe. Couldn't you go down to the Dower House and talk to him? I could ring him up and you'll be met. They're wonderful people and I know you'll like

Anthony. If you can't do anything yourself, perhaps you could recommend one of those agencies.''

The appeal in the young man's eyes weakened Forsythe's resolve. That startling resemblance to Sandy, the barrister thought. ''Very well. You make the arrangements and I'll speak with your friend. But do remember, Buffy, no promises.''

Buffy sprang to his feet. ''I don't know how to thank you, Mr. Forsythe.''

''You can start by calling me Robert.'' Forsythe chuckled. ''And, when you become a full-fledged physician, I'll take it out in free appointments. By the way, Sandy says you intend to specialize. Which field of medicine is it to be?''

The boy walked a few feet to the nearest rubbish bin—plastic, of course—and dumped the contents of the tray. When he turned, his eyes were dancing. ''Obstetrics. To collect on that debt, it looks like you must marry.''

''I may do just that.'' Forsythe led the way to the door, glad to leave the noisy place. Outside, a fine rain was falling and he took a deep breath of cool moist air. In contrast to the din of the restaurant, the rumble of traffic sounded almost harmonious. He turned to his companion. ''Thanks for the meal, Buffy, and give my love to Sandy.''

''I'll do that. Oh, one moment. Aunt Abigail sent a message. She said to tell you to pick up something for her TLC. What's that supposed to mean. Tender loving care?''

''Hardly. Your aunt has a new hobby. Didn't she tell you about it?''

''I knew she was taking Spanish lessons but that's hardly new. She said you collect jade. Is she making some kind of collection?''

''Indeed she is, but trust Sandy to collect unusual objects. TLC stands for Tawdry Ludicrous Collection. It started when one of her many nieces brought her a souvenir from Paris. Quite a lovely little thing. The Eiffel Tower fashioned from crystal and filled with perfume.''

Golden light from the neon bars fell across the younger man's puzzled face. ''That hardly sounds tawdry or ludicrous.''

Forsythe grinned. "The perfume was made in Munich and the container in Venice."

"Ah, the light dawns."

"Then a friend made a trip to Canada and brought Sandy back a piggy bank shaped like a Mountie, complete with red coat and horse. This item was made in Taiwan. That started Sandy on her collection. Now she hounds everyone to keep an eye out for similar souvenirs. So far, the star of her collection is a replica of the Taj Mahal that squirts catsup. Purchased in Agra and manufactured in Japan. But I don't think I'll be able to come up with anything in a quiet English village to challenge those gems."

"You never know what might pop up in a quiet English village," Buford Sanderson said darkly. "Remember Miss Marple."

Through the nightmarish days to follow, those words would return to haunt Robert Forsythe.

CHAPTER TWO

AFTER SETTING DOWN HIS PIGSKIN TRAVELING CASE, Forsythe turned to help a plump, pretty woman down onto the station platform. She needed all the help he could give her. Not only did she have two bulging suitcases but a basket, a small cardboard box, and two children. The one she was holding out to the barrister was a tiny girl, barely toddling and speaking some language only her mother seemed to understand. The boy looked about eight and needed no help. He leaped down and stood by Forsythe, gazing balefully up at him. Forsythe had heard the boy speak only once and his accent appeared to try to echo the western outfit he was wearing. The child wore a coonskin cap, fringed jacket, cowboy boots, and jeans. From his lean hips, two holsters swung, the handles of toy six-guns protruding.

With one hand, Forsythe held the squirming toddler; with the other, he lifted down a suitcase and then the basket. The boy watched but made no move to assist. "Here," his beleaguered mother snapped. "Lend a hand, Ronnie. Take the box."

The only part that moved on Ronnie was his lips. They curled into a sneer while Forsythe handled the box and then handed the toddler to her mother. "Awfully good of you," the lady told the barrister, and gave her son a shove. "At least you can find your Aunt Ruthie."

11

Ronnie drawled, "She's aheadin' this way, pardner."

Ruthie, florid face beaming welcome, was indeed hurrying to meet the little party. She bore a striking resemblance to Ronnie's mother but she was older and pleasing plumpness had disappeared under layers of fat. The two women fell into an embrace, crushing the toddler between two imposing sets of breasts. The child started to howl, and Forsythe, his duty done, moved down the platform.

He swept an approving glance over the ancient station house. It was built of clapboard and although it could have used a coat of paint, it still had the charm of a bygone era. This small station, Forsythe mused, would soon be abandoned and the branch train he had arrived on would disappear. This was happening all over England: a pity, but it was all supposed to be in the name of progress.

Over his head, banging and clattering in the wind, a weather-beaten sign announced this was indeed Safrone. He glanced at a dusty sedan drawn up beside the platform, wondering whether this could be the vehicle that had been promised for him. However, Ruthie, now carrying the toddler and one of the suitcases, was waddling toward the sedan, followed by Mother, laden with the rest of the luggage. The boy still stood straddle-legged, squinting up at Forsythe.

"Come along, Ronnie," Ruthie called from the car. "I'm giving your mum a cup of tea and I got biscuits for you and Sally." She waved a thermos and a paper bag enticingly, but the boy, one hand hovering over a six-gun, showed no interest in biscuits.

Forsythe smiled down at Ronnie, wondering what the child was seeing in his imagination—certainly not a station platform; more likely, visions of the American frontier: sheriffs, Indian chiefs, outlaws, deeds of valor with blazing six-guns. . . .

The shriek of brakes wrenched him from his own dream pictures and he looked around and saw a low-slung silver car drawing in beside the sedan where Ruthie and her sister were sipping tea and nibbling biscuits. The silver door opened and a man hopped out and walked toward the platform. "Mr. Forsythe, I presume," he called.

12

The barrister nodded and the man made a graceful and sweeping bow. "Felipe Manuel Jesus Delcardo, at your service. Known to all and sundry as Tip, which I prefer. I've kept you waiting."

"Not for long." Forsythe bent for his case but the newcomer plucked it up.

Tip's appearance matched his long musical Latin name. He looked to be in his early twenties, was considerably shorter than Forsythe but much heavier, and had a wide olive-skinned face and a shaggy head of black hair. From that swarthy face beamed a pair of the most brilliant blue eyes that Forsythe had ever seen.

Those eyes moved from the barrister to the motionless boy. "Who is your little amigo?"

"A traveling companion. Ronnie, say hello to Tip."

Ronnie contented himself with a steely glance that swept up Tip's jeans and denim jacket and fastened on the broad face.

Patting the coonskin cap, Tip asked jovially, "And who are you supposed to be? Wyatt Earp?"

The boy's lips barely moved. "Davy Crockett, hombre."

"Ah, the king of the wild frontier." White teeth flashed in a smile and, lowering his voice, he said to Forsythe, "Watch this. I'll show you how much these kids actually know about American history." He spread his free arm wide. "If you're Crockett, that makes me General Santa Anna."

"That makes you *dead*." The boy's hand moved and he leveled a six-gun. "Remember the Alamo!" he shouted, and pulled the trigger. A stream of water flashed from the barrel directly into the startled face of the erstwhile Santa Anna.

"Why you little son of—"

"Easy!" Forsythe grabbed Tip's denim-clad arm. "History test over and it looks like Ronnie just made an *A*."

Pulling out a handkerchief, Tip mopped at his dripping face while Ronnie grimly watched, a hand grasping the handle of the other six-gun. "Better watch it! I still got a full load here and I don't fire blanks!"

"Ronnie!" His mother was galloping toward them. "*You naughty boy*. Look what you did to the gentleman." She seized her son's shoulder in a plump hand. "I'm *so* sorry. Ronnie means no harm, you know. I blame it all on that telly."

Tip seemed incapable of responding and it was Forsythe who said genially, "No harm done. The attack was provoked, so don't be hard on the lad."

As she hauled Davy Crockett away, Tip muttered, "I'd like about five minutes alone with that gringo. Ah, well, let's get on to the Dower House."

He led the way toward the car and Forsythe followed. Tip slung the traveling case in the backseat and held the door for the barrister. The silver Jaguar reversed, made a turn, and glided away from the station. Forsythe glanced at his companion. "How far to the Dower House?"

"About six miles. That's the village of Safrone dead ahead. Population about two hundred, counting dogs, and the house is five miles beyond it."

"And your position in the household is?"

"Factotum, majordomo, sometimes called house*boy* by my master, Mr. Funicelli. Actually captive serf, bought and paid for by said master."

"Come now. If I remember correctly, slavery was abolished over a century ago."

"Better tell that to Mr. Funicelli. No kidding, Mr. Forsythe, he actually *bought* me."

The barrister eyed the younger man's profile. "Perhaps you'd better explain."

"It's no secret. Mr. Funicelli is proud of his bargain. He was traveling in Mexico with a companion, an American engineer. They were there on business, something about oil exploration. Their jeep broke down near the village where my family and I lived. While they were waiting for repairs, Mr. Funicelli saw me, decided what he wanted was a miniature Hispanic houseboy, and struck a bargain with my mother and father."

"Money changed hands?"

"Enough to make my family figure *they*'d struck oil. Mr. Funicelli promised them he'd see I was educated and would have me become a U.S. citizen, so when the jeep left Quila, I went along with the rest of the baggage.''

"I can hardly believe this.''

"I know.'' Brilliant blue eyes left the road and swept over the barrister's well-cut tweeds and rolled-necked sweater. "People like you have no comprehension what genuine poverty is all about. My parents figured they were doing the best not only for the rest of my family but also for me. The year before this transaction, a polio epidemic had swept through Quila and it left my father very frail and with a crippled leg. My brother, Carlos, the baby, was crippled by polio, too. When Mr. Funicelli hove into view, the Delcardo family was starving. And I don't mean hungry. I mean *starving*.''

"Did Mr. Funicelli keep his promises?''

"The master always keeps his promises. Prides himself on it.''

"Well . . .'' Forsythe fumbled for words. "How old were you?''

"Twelve.''

Ye gods, Forsythe thought. Aloud, he said, "If you don't want to stay in his employ, I don't suppose you have to. After all, freedom and liberty are your adopted country's watchwords.''

A bitter smile twitched the other man's lips. "Haven't you heard . . . 'Freedom's just another word for nothing left to lose'? I've still something to lose, Mr. Forsythe, take my word for it.''

Feeling distinctly uncomfortable about these confidences concerning his host, the barrister changed the subject. "Pretty country. How did the Funicellis select this area?''

"The name.''

"I beg your pardon?''

"The master was cruising the byways seeking a suitable home for his future bride when he saw a signpost with the name Safrone on it. His grandfather and his mother came from a hamlet in Sicily called Saffrona. He must have figured it was a sign from heaven, because he immediately checked out the real estate in the area. The local squire, who just happens to be chief constable, had a chunk of land and a

15

house he wanted to sell. Funicelli bought it and, after suitable alterations had been made, he brought his bride to the Dower House. Sir Cecil Safrone, the squire, and Mr. Funicelli struck a gentleman's agreement that the grounds and the exterior of the place were to be left much the same, so only the interior was changed and a couple of wings were added." Tip flashed his white grin. "I can hardly wait for you to see it. And . . . here we are."

The car swung smoothly between gateposts and passed a sprawling stone cottage with bare rose vines twining around the doorway and windows. The twisting drive was flanked by ancient oaks, meeting overhead in a tangle of naked branches. At the foot of the trees huddled rhododendrons, their buds still tightly closed. Then the Jaguar rounded the final curve and Forsythe caught sight of a charming manor, not overly large but built of rose-colored brick with flashings of white stone outlining the windows. Ivy crowded in profusion over the brick but had been neatly trimmed away from windows and doors. The area in front of the house was graveled and looked as though it had recently been raked over.

"Certainly well cared for," Robert told his companion.

"Practically manicured by the gardeners. They were originally retainers of Sir Cecil's and live in that cottage we passed by the gate. The brawny sons pamper the grounds and Mrs. Dour acts as housekeeper and part-time cook."

"An odd name."

Tip laughed. "Their name is actually Flower but Dour fits better. Except for the Flower daughter, who was housemaid for a time. She's gone now but, believe me, she deserved the name."

He pulled the car to a stop before the imposing door and Forsythe got out and stretched. He looked up at the ivy-covered facade. "You mentioned wings had been added."

Tip was pulling out the barrister's case. "Have a look down the side of the house.

Forsythe did that. He took a casual look and then stared. Joined on to the old brick of the manor was a long stucco wall in an appalling shade of pink. It was unbroken by windows, had a metal stairway leading up to a door, and was high enough to contain two floors. He called over his shoulder, "Is that monstrosity built right across the rear, and where are the windows?"

"It's in two sections. Brackets a courtyard. The windows overlook that." Tip unlocked the door. "Come have a gander at Funicelli's Folly. Somewhere between California Horrible and Club Med."

Forsythe paused to admire the fine hand-carved door. Then he stepped past it and stopped in his tracks. "Ye gods!" he blurted.

CHAPTER THREE

"**C**OME NOW," TIP CHIDED. "A LAWYER SHOULD BE able to do better than that. After all, words are your business. Come down to the middle of this . . . whatever it is, and have another try."

Forsythe followed his guide across a wide landing covered with a carpet so thick he felt as though he was wading, down three shallow steps, and across more luxurious gray carpeting.

Tip flipped a hand. "This is called the conversation pit. Best thing to do is stand near the fireplace and slowly revolve."

The fireplace was freestanding, with a raised hearth and a copper conical fire hood suspended over it. The circular conversation pit, at first glance, looked about the size of a soccer field and was dotted with groups of armchairs and lounges all covered in butter-colored leather. There were dozens of small tables of some rich dark wood, possibly teak.

Taking Tip's advice, the barrister slowly revolved. Three sides of the pit were surrounded by a curved wide platform divided into sections by fanciful screens. No two screens seemed to be the same. There were a number of Oriental silk ones either painted or embroidered, a couple of carved wooden ones, one that looked like a filigree of jade, and another atrocious one that resembled beaten gold but was possibly brass.

Tip was grinning from ear to ear. "Looks like a dollhouse, doesn't it?"

It did resemble a gigantic dollhouse. The three-sided sections varied in furnishings. The one closest to a door that probably led into a wing was obviously a formal dining room. The next one, divided by an Oriental screen, was less formal but had a dining table and chairs—perhaps a breakfast room. There was a huge area with bookcases towering against the outer wall and featuring an immense leather-topped desk. Yet another section contained a billiard table and several slot machines.

Tip asked mockingly. "Any words yet, Mr. Forsythe?"

The barrister shook his head and glanced up. Far above was what appeared to be the original roof of the manor, crisscrossed with ancient rafters. Between these rafters were any number of skylights. Dragging his eyes down, he continued to revolve. At the rear end of the conversation pit, three shallow steps led to a platform that ran the full width of the house. Above it was a wide balcony with an ornamental railing. His eyes fastened on a huge object resting on the platform and he blinked.

"That, Mr. Forsythe, is the pièce de résistance. Designed by Mr. Funicelli and constructed exactly to his order."

For a moment, the barrister couldn't figure out what the hell the thing was. Then he realized it must be a lift, but what a lift! It was shaped like a bird cage. Hundreds of delicate brass strands wove an intricate pattern and the interior looked like a lady's jewel case, complete with a pink velvet bench.

The barrister was still speechless. He wished Sandy was with him. Her acerbic wit would have soon put this weird place into perspective. As he thought of his secretary, words finally came. "Tawdry," he muttered, "and utterly ludicrous."

"*Wonderful,*" the houseman exclaimed. "I *knew* you could do it. 'Tawdry' and 'ludicrous' are perfect. The best

19

I've ever done are 'ridiculous' and 'disgusting.' I also like the expression on your face. A blend of complete disbelief and icy British hauteur."

Turning away from the lift, Forsythe gazed around. "This house must be eighteenth century. What, in the name of all that's holy, did they do to it?"

"Gutted it. Tore out floors, walls, charming old rooms, and put in supports. In time, they produced what you're looking at. Mr. Funicelli kept his promise not to do much to the exterior, but he went to town in here. Turned the whole house into one room and stuck on the wings for other quarters. He couldn't touch the original windows, so he had those skylights installed. Incidentally, he's very proud of his work, boasts he did a better job than an architect could have."

"No architect in his right mind would have touched this . . . this desecration," Forsythe said wrathfully. "And not only is that lift unsightly but what purpose does it serve? As far as I can tell, it only goes up to the balcony."

"Mr. Funicelli insists that's for his pampered bride's convenience, but she never uses it. In fact, the only person who does is the master. He hates exercise and when his mother, who dotes on exercise and urges it on her son, isn't around, Mr. Funicelli rides up and down like a bird in a gilded cage."

Forsythe's eyes coldly fixed on the younger man. "You have a habit of speaking very casually and slightingly of your employer and his family."

"For a humble peon, eh?" Tip set down the traveling case and stretched. His denim jacket fell open and under it an ornate gold crucifix dangled against a white T-shirt. "And you're putting me in my proper place. I assure you my present manner and confidences are for you only. With the Funicelli family, I am suitably subservient, to say nothing of servile. A classic case of a split personality.

"Did you display this side to Buffy?"

"Señor Buford Sanderson? Perish the thought."

"Then why with me?"

20

"Because not only do I like you but you happen to be what I'm going to be in time . . . a lawyer. When we return to the States, I'll be taking a night course that will turn me into a second Clarence Darrow."

"Such modesty." Forsythe smiled. "But, obviously, your master does keep his promises. He's given you a first-rate education. By the way, how did you get your nickname?"

"Mr. Funicelli said that was the first English word I learned. As in gratuity." He slumped his shoulders, lowered his head, and held out a palm. "Tip, por favor, señor."

"I'll give you a tip right now." Forsythe jerked his head toward the balcony. "Better slip into your other personality. I've a hunch that's your master."

"So it is. Watch this peon closely."

The man on the balcony ignored the lift and trotted over to the staircase that led down to the platform. "No," Tip whispered. "Not Mr. Funicelli. He isn't using the lift and Mama Rosa is nowhere in sight. That's the master's cousin and look-alike."

The man stepped onto the landing and headed for the steps leading down to the conversation pit. "Hi, there! Nice to meet you." He extended a hand. "I'm Anthony's cousin, Fredo Clemenza. How was your trip?"

"Enjoyable, Mr. Clemenza."

"Better make that Fredo. We don't bother with formality around here."

Forsythe caught himself in time. He'd been about to mention he'd noticed that with the Mexican houseman. Instead, he contented himself with looking his host's cousin over. Fredo Clemenza was about Tip's height but he was heavier, with wide shoulders and a barrel-shaped chest. He looked in his fifties and his black hair was beautifully styled, his features massive, and under thick black brows were magnificent dark eyes.

Those eyes flicked toward the manservant. "Don't stand around, Tip. Get that case up to Mr. Forsythe's room."

"Si, señor." Tip took a couple of steps and then paused. "Is Señor Funicelli free? If he is, I'll show Señor Forsythe up to the office."

21

Clemenza spoke directly to the barrister. "Anthony is eager to meet you, Robert, but I'm afraid there'll be a short delay. He's in the midst of a conference call with some of his people in Los Angeles, Chicago, New York. I'd like to stay with you myself but I have to run into the village and pick up the mail. Tip can show you to your quarters, or perhaps you'd prefer to wait in the courtyard. The twins are out there and they'll entertain you."

Forsythe opted for the courtyard, and Clemenza pointed a stubby finger under the balcony. "Door's right back there. I'll see you later, Robert. Have the twins give you a drink. Tip, you check with Mr. Funicelli in about twenty minutes and see if he's free. And don't let him see you in those clothes. You know how he feels about them!"

"Si, señor," Tip said humbly. "I will change immediately."

As he passed the Mexican, Forsythe shot an amazed glance at him. There was no trace of the cocky young man who had brought him from the station. Talk about split personalities.

He located the glass doors and, to his amusement, one slid silently open as he approached, very much as the door had at the hamburger restaurant he'd visited with Buffy. By this time, Forsythe considered he was immune to further shocks, but outside that door, another was waiting.

He stepped from a comfortable house temperature into a tropical heat wave. In the courtyard, the cool and moist English spring didn't hold sway. Through a glass roof fully two stories above, light streamed down on an area that reminded him of the French Riviera. Palm trees, bushes flowering in gaudy colors, fine white sand, and an expanse of blue water in a fair-sized lagoon spread back to a stucco wall centered with a stout wooden door. On both sides were pink stucco wings, their facades, on two stories, broken by numerous glass doors. The upper story had a balcony railed in white wrought iron. Here, the glaring pink of the walls wasn't as obtrusive. Purple and white bougainvillea flowered profusely, mercifully hiding much of the hideous stucco.

22

Finding the heat and myriad perfumes nearly overwhelming, Forsythe looked around for a seat. Arranged in groups were white wrought-iron tables supporting pink and white umbrellas and ringed by white chairs. As he sank down at a table close to the lagoon, he decided he was still at a loss for words. He also decided he had sand in one shoe. How many American dollars, he wondered, had it taken to create this place? And where are the Funicelli twins who are going to give me a large and much-needed drink?"

"Welcome to the Gingerbread House," a voice called.

He spotted the source of the welcome. To his left, two bodies sprawled facedown on beach towels. Both were young, bronzed, lithe, and appeared to be wearing only tiny white bikini bottoms. The triangles were sodden with moisture and water drops spangled the brown backs. Both boys? No, Buffy had clearly said a boy and a girl. From this angle, the twins looked identical. The voice could have been a fairly deep feminine one or a rather light male one.

He decided on a direct approach. "Fredo said you could provide me with a drink."

"Anything your heart desires, Roger—"

"Robert. Robert Forsythe."

"The bar's near the big palm. If you don't want alcohol, there're lemonade and coffee."

The bar was also made of white iron and held every variety of alcohol one could wish. Ignoring the lemonade and coffee, the barrister poured a generous amount of Glenfiddich and waded through sand back to the table. The twins hadn't moved a muscle.

"Do you have names?" he asked.

One figure stirred, flopped over, and sat up. Ah, the Funicelli son. "I'm Hansel and this rude creature is my sister, Gretchen, who can never remember names."

"No ruder than you and at least I remember faces." The other twin turned over, sat up, and managed to drag the towel so it modestly covered her from brown shoulders to small sand-encrusted feet.

23

Hansel and Gretchen were not identical, of course, but there was certainly a strong likeness. They had heart-shaped faces, fine brows, and huge brown eyes reminiscent of their cousin Fredo's. They appeared to emphasize that resemblance in their hair-styles, flaxen hair cropped short like dandelions running to seed. The boy's features were coarser and his chin was heavier.

The girl was regarding Forsythe with interest. "How do you like Father Funicelli's idea of ye olde English home?"

The barrister had been applying himself to Glenfiddich. He set down the glass and said evasively, "It doesn't seem to afford much privacy."

"The wings do." Hansel waved a languid hand. "That's where we take refuge when we're not basking here. Actually, when you get used to it, this courtyard is quite pleasant. You're not dressed for it. Why don't you make yourself comfortable? There're oodles of trunks in that cabana back there."

Forsythe cast a longing look at the blue lagoon. He could feel sweat trickling down his back. He compromised by slipping off his tweed jacket. "Thanks for the offer, but I'll be seeing your father shortly and I hardly think he'd welcome a guest in trunks and dripping wet."

"He'd love it," Gretchen said flatly. "He prides himself on being democratic. With his peer group, that is. Menials had better know their places or else."

The towel had inched down and the barrister caught a glimpse of the curve of a small breast. "Gingerbread House," he murmured. "Hansel and Gretchen."

"Our mother picked the names. She was a Bavarian," Hansel told him.

"Have you left a trail of bread crumbs behind you?"

Gretchen's dark eyes moodily regarded him. "Haven't you heard, Roger—"

"Robert."

"That you can never go home?"

"Where do you live? Chicago? California?"

"Vermont. We have a few acres there and—"

24

"We raise vegetables," her brother chimed in. "And we have a couple of Jersey cows and some hens and beehives. We sell produce to earn our daily bread."

"Considering your background, I should hardly think that necessary."

"Considering we won't take any of the Funicellis' blood-soaked money, it's essential," Gretchen said and then giggled. "You know what he's thinking, Hansel? That big daddy must be a don for the Mafia. Not that kind of blood. Have you ever visited a slaughterhouse, Roger . . . pardon me . . . Robert? No? If you ever had, you might never touch meat again. Father wanted to show us how humane the modern methods of butchering food animals are and so he forced us to visit one of his plants. At the time we were seven—"

"Eight," her brother said.

"Whatever. Anyway, we never again ate meat. And, remember, the Funicelli fortune is firmly based on murdering helpless animals." The towel had slipped farther and she paused to adjust it. "You ask a lot of questions, but I suppose in your business, that's an occupational hazard. Or, I should say, both your businesses. Lawyer and sleuth. What a combination. And exactly what does Father want with you?"

"Hasn't he told you?"

Hansel shook his flaxen head. "He claims he wants to meet a modern Sherlock. But Father is a genuine Sicilian. More twists to him than to a rattlesnake."

His sister ran her fingers through her spiked hair. "Better watch yourself. This is one snake that doesn't rattle before it strikes."

Hansel made a sound much like his sister's giggle. "What Robert is now thinking is that we aren't dutiful children and that we bad-mouth our daddy."

"Who just happens to be the wicked witch rattler," Gretchen muttered.

Forsythe looked from one face to the other. "In the Gingerbread House, the witch was a woman."

Winking a long-lashed eye, Hansel said, "Sherlocks should know witches come in both sexes."

25

What I'd like to do, Forsythe thought, is to take both of you over my knee and tan your already-tanned bottoms. How old were they? he wondered. They had to be Buffy's age, around twenty-two, but they seemed much younger.

His thoughts were interrupted by Tip's voice. "Señor Forsythe, Señor Funicelli is free now."

As Forsythe rose, the twins flopped back on their bellies. One of them, possibly the boy, called, "Tip, how about mixing up some fresh lemonade?"

"Si, Señor Hansel. As soon as I escort Señor Forsythe to your father's office."

Forsythe slung his jacket over an arm and waded to the glass door. He stamped sand from his shoes and stepped into welcome coolness. Tip asked jovially, "Warm enough for you?"

He had not only changed his personality but his appearance. Now he wore black trousers and a spotless white mess jacket. His unruly hair was parted in the middle and slicked back from his brow. Forsythe decided that the houseman now bore a startling resemblance to a thirties bandleader.

Forsythe found his handkerchief and mopped at his dripping face. "It's a sweatbox out there but still preferable to this house. Where did the 'si, señor' act go?"

"Only disappeared for the moment. In a short time, I'll be cringing again. The master prefers his houseboy to be heavily and meekly Hispanic. What a crock of shit!"

"Tsk, tsk! I hardly think Clarence Darrow talked like that."

"This one does. Like to jump on the lift?"

"I think I can manage the stairs, Tip."

"And how did the twins strike you?"

The barrister slipped on his jacket. "I don't trust first impressions." He waited a moment and then he said, "Drop the other shoe, Tip, and make some snide remark about them."

"Nothing I can say. A case of empathy, I guess. We all loathe the same man."

26

"If they feel that way about their father, why are they here?"

"Mama Rosa insisted, and even the twins obey her."

"A matriarch?"

"The best type. A nice lady."

"Now you are shocking me. Do you realize that's the first time I've heard you compliment a Funicelli?"

Tip's white grin flashed. "Hold on to those words. It may be the last time." He waved a hand toward the curving staircase. "After you."

When Forsythe reached the balcony, he paused to glance at the gate in the metal railing, which apparently slid aside when the lift rose into position. He glanced over his shoulder. At the far end of the balcony was a heavy door with lighted red lights over it announcing this was the exit. At the other end of the balcony was its twin.

"Fire exits," his guide explained. "So the household can bolt down metal stairs in case of a conflagration. Luckily, this peon's quarters are on the lower floor near the kitchen. All I'd have to do is cast my body through patio doors into the courtyard." He touched the barrister's sleeve. "Orientation time. East wing down there. Entrance to upper west wing back there. In the lower east, Mama Rosa has her suite and there are also assorted guest rooms. On its upper floor, the twins have their hideaway, and you'll be in there near them. West wing lower is the kitchen, various offices, and the humble peon's room. Upper west is the residence of the master and his blushing bride. Comprehend, amigo?"

"Clear as a bell. But where does Fredo Clemenza have his quarters?"

"Mr. Clemenza doesn't live in the house. He has a cottage on the estate. Unlike his cousin, he enjoys exercise and it's a fair walk back and forth from this house to his cottage."

"And the master's office . . ."

"Opens off this balcony directly across from where the passengers disembark from the lift. Next door to it is the

27

master's private lounging room." Tip tapped on the office door and from behind it came a baritone rumble. Swinging it open, Tip said in a hushed voice, "Señor Forsythe."

A man rose from behind a steel desk, circled it, and extended a hand. "Sorry to have kept you waiting, Robert. Business, you know. Even here, I'm never free of it."

The barrister's slender hand was engulfed in a powerful clasp and he exchanged pleasantries with the master of the Dower House. He could see why Tip had momentarily mistaken Fredo Clemenza for his cousin. Not only did they have the same build and coloring but they were wearing similar clothes—tan slacks, a camel jacket, a pale yellow shirt open at the throat, revealing a mat of black hair.

"One moment, Tip," Funicelli ordered. "Would you care for a drink, Robert?"

"Just had one with your children."

"Ah, you've met the twins. I rather wish that could have been delayed until I had a chance to prepare you. Come to think of it, I don't understand them myself." Funicelli gave a deep chuckle. "I suppose that's been parents' complaints down through the ages. The younger generation! Tip, find out if Fredo is back with the mail yet."

Tip had no chance to respond. Fredo brushed past the Mexican and extended a bulging manila envelope. "Got it right here, Anthony. Quite a batch today."

As Funicelli opened the envelope, Forsythe eyed one cousin and then the other. When they were together, the resemblance was less striking. Clemenza, beside his cousin, was only a negative beside a full-colored print. Funicelli had the bearing, the aura, the sense of tightly leashed power. His mouth was firmer, his square chin had a deep cleft, his dark eyes were wider spaced.

Funicelli waved an imperious hand. "Off you both go. Robert, do be seated. Have you had a chance to look around the Dower House? Yes? What do you think?"

"It's highly unusual," Forsythe said sincerely. "I've never seen anything to compare."

The firm mouth curled into a smile. Apparently, the creator of the house was accepting this as a compliment. He sank into his swivel chair and crossed one ankle over a knee. "I've often thought that if I hadn't been tied to my father's business, I'd have excelled at architecture. I pride myself on my flair for it."

"Did you design your other homes?"

"Both the family home in Chicago and the ranch house in California were built long before I was born, and Mother, bless her, hasn't let me update either. Odd, Mama Rosa is such a modern woman and yet she simply detests this house. Insists the only reason she consents to stay here is because of Lucia. My wife, as Buffy may have mentioned, is pregnant and Mama Rosa is hovering over her. That's Lucia right there."

Forsythe had already noticed Lucia. In his office, Funicelli had managed to control his impulse toward fantastic expression. The room was merely functional. The desk, filing cabinets, and chairs were constructed of gray-painted steel. One side table supported a manual typewriter that looked older than its owner; another was covered with various telephones. The sole spot of color was a painting, flanked by gold crucifixes, on the wall directly in front of Forsythe. A girl was painted standing by what looked like a village well. A loose rather virginal white garment fell around her body in graceful folds to small bare feet. Her black hair flowed like a lustrous veil around her face and shoulders. She had ripe pouting lips and the wonderful dark eyes of the Funicelli family. In fact, Forsythe thought, the girl looked like a relation of the man facing him. "Your wife is lovely," he murmured.

The deep chuckle sounded again. "And no doubt you're thinking much too young for this old codger. And you could be right. Lucia is younger than Gretchen and Hansel. But the Funicellis, like many families, have traditions. Lucia is a distant cousin and Mama Rosa was a distant cousin of my father's. Mother was only sixteen when Father—and at the time he was my age—sent to Saffrona for a bride. Their marriage was indeed blessed in heaven, and I fully expect mine to be, too."

Despite this confident statement, he sounded a trifle defensive. Forsythe changed the subject. "I understand you purchased this house from the chief constable. Has he seen the renovations?"

"Indeed he has. Sir Cecil dines with us frequently and he seems quite overwhelmed at the changes. He's not an effusive man but his remarks were similar to yours. Sir Cecil did mention he was happy I was a man of my word and had kept the grounds and the front of the house as it was when his mother lived here. Sentiment, I suppose. Many of the Safrone widows have lived in this house. But Sir Cecil is a childless widower and his family line, sadly, is ended." Funicelli sighed. "Sic gloria transit."

Forsythe nearly sighed, too. He was tired, his bad knee was aching, and he felt grubby. He wriggled his toes and sand grated in one shoe. "Perhaps," he suggested, "we can get to the purpose of this meeting, Mr. Funicelli."

"Please call me Anthony. As Buffy may also have told you, I insist on informality. Fine lad, Buffy. A nephew of your secretary, I understand. I would dearly like to meet Miss Sanderson, but Buffy assured me his aunt is caring for his mother and her family. Buffy is such a refreshing boy, so well mannered, and respectful of his elders. Strange, I don't really like children and yet I took to Buffy immediately."

An odd remark, Forsythe thought, from a man with two grown children and a bride pregnant with a third. "You don't like children?"

"I know it's not a popular sentiment, but I never have. And yet children adore me. Climb all over me like puppies."

"Somewhat like cats, I suppose. I've a friend who loathes cats and yet every feline that comes near him tries to jump on his lap."

"Exactly." Removing his ankle from his knee, Funicelli bent over the desk. "Robert, exactly what did Buffy tell you?"

Forsythe debated for a moment and then said bluntly, "He senses you're afraid of something and may need help."

"Afraid? Ridiculous! I've never felt fear in my life! It looks as though Buffy has given you an erroneous impression. Granted, when he was here, I was disturbed about . . . well, it was connected with one of my business concerns. Serious enough at the time, but it has since been resolved. I think, Robert, that Buffy sent you down here on a wild-goose chase."

All of which fails to explain, Forsythe thought, why you reached for a weapon when Buffy entered this room suddenly. "Then why," he asked evenly, "were you so insistent on meeting me?"

"Insistent? Rather a strong term. I merely indicated to Buffy that I should like to make your acquaintance." Settling back comfortably, Funicelli continued. "I've read and reread Sir Conan Doyle's masterpieces and I'm a Sherlock Holmes's buff. I've also read the accounts of all your cases and you sound like that famous detective. And Miss Sanderson reminds me of the faithful Dr. Watson."

"I'm glad Sandy didn't hear that remark," the barrister said. "She draws that comparison often herself. Only she calls Watson a bumbling idiot, trailing after Holmes, making notes and asinine remarks. So . . . you simply wanted a firsthand account of our work." Anger stirred. "I should think a man in your position would understand another busy person."

"That goes without saying."

"This wild-goose chase, as you call it, has wrenched me away from my chambers, my work. I've had to relegate a brief to a junior who already is carrying a heavy work load."

Funicelli reached for an ebony box, lifted the lid, and mutely offered a cigar to his guest. When the younger man shook his head, Funicelli selected one and rolled it between his palms. "Put like that, it does make me sound thoughtless. But I did so want to meet you and—"

"We could have met in London," Forsythe said icily. "Had lunch or dinner together."

"And that's what I should have arranged. Robert, I apologize. But now that you are here, I must try and make amends. Surely you can take a couple of days and enjoy. I've provided everything for guests' amusement, such as swimming, games—"

"I don't wish to be amused." Forsythe was on his feet. "I'll accept your hospitality tonight, but in the morning I'll return to London."

"As you wish. If you like, I can have Tip drive you back to the city."

"I'll take the train."

Unperturbed, Funicelli picked up the manila envelope. "Well, at least we'll have dinner and the evening. I've rung for Tip. He'll show you to your room. Dinner will be at eight but come down a bit early and have a drink and meet the rest of my family. Be sure to wear something cooler. I'm doing the cooking tonight and dinner will be served in the courtyard."

A soft tap resounded on the door, it opened, and Tip humbly awaited his master's commands. "Take Mr. Forsythe to his quarters. Until dinner, Robert."

As they left the room, Funicelli was sorting his mail into piles. Inwardly fuming, the barrister followed Tip along the balcony toward the east wing. The arrogance of the man, he thought angrily. No, that wasn't the right word. Anthony Funicelli's attitude far surpassed arrogance. Divine right of kings? Closer but still not on target. Tip had been correct. For a person whose profession relied on a command of words, he was dolefully lacking in them this day.

As Tip opened the heavy door leading to the wing, a voice called Forsythe's name. He turned and saw Funicelli standing on the balcony outside his office. His face was in shadow but there was an odd note in his voice. "Would you be kind enough to come back, Robert?"

"I understood our conversation was concluded."

Funicelli lifted an imploring hand. "Something's come up. Please."

Forsythe shrugged, feeling the sweat-soaked wool of his sweater sliding over his shoulder blades. As he slowly retraced his steps, he wondered whether his host was about to suggest another amusing game.

The game Anthony Funicelli had in mind was far from amusing. It was deadly.

CHAPTER FOUR

FORSYTHE LOWERED HIS GAZE FROM LUCIA FUNICELLI'S painted face to her husband's somber real-life one. With one hand, the older man toyed with an ebony-handled, long-bladed paper knife. With the other, he touched a corner of an envelope. The remainder of the mail was swept into an untidy heap by one edge of the desk.

"Second thoughts?" Forsythe asked.

Funicelli nodded and started to shove the envelope toward his guest. Then his hand stilled. He said slowly, "Before you see this, I'd better fill you in. As you know, Lucia is my second wife. My first, a German girl I met in Munich, was totally unlike Lucia. Ilse was one of those brawny athletic types with flaxen hair and blue eyes. My mother realized long before I did that the marriage had been a mistake. I was infatuated with Ilse and she was infatuated with the Funicelli millions. Shortly before the twins were born, our marriage broke up. I settled a generous amount of money on Ilse and didn't argue about custody of the babies. As far as I was concerned, she could have them."

"Did you divorce?"

Funicelli swiveled his chair around and pointed an expressive finger at the crucifixes. "We couldn't. Ilse and I were both Catholic and, although I'm not devout, my mother certainly is. Mama Rosa would never consider divorce. So I became a grass widower and that went on for years. When the twins were seven, Mama Rosa retrieved them from my estranged wife and when they were eleven, Ilse died while visiting the children at our ranch in California. Mama Rosa started agitating for me to marry again, to produce a suitable heir to the Funicelli empire, but this was one time I failed to be an obedient son. I'd had enough of wives and children and—"

"You already had a son," Forsythe pointed out.

A faint smile twisted the corners of Funicelli's lips. "I said suitable. Hansel can hardly be called that. Mother wants a grandson similar to me, to my father. Who Hansel takes after, I've no idea. He's unlike Ilse and certainly nothing like me. Must be a throwback."

Forsythe nodded and then said, "If you don't mind, I think I can use a drink."

His host pulled himself up and opened the steel door of a cabinet, disclosing a small fridge. "Afraid all I keep here is bourbon. Would you like me to have Tip—"

"Bourbon will do. Neat please." Funicelli was lifting out a bowl of ice cubes. "No ice."

"I seldom touch this stuff, but right now I can use a drink, too." He handed the barrister a glass and carried another one, this one tinkling ice cubes, back to his chair. "Where was I?"

"A widower resisting his mother's desire for a grandson."

"Sounds a bit like a soap opera, doesn't it?" Funicelli sipped his bourbon and shuddered. "But then life is much like a soap. Twisted relationships, twisted emotions. To get on with my personal soap: About two and a half years ago, Mother had an illness that left her weak and run-down. Her physician suggested she convalesce in a warmer, drier climate and so she decided to visit her childhood home in Sicily. At the same time, Lucia was in Saffrona on vacation from her convent school. Mother decided that Lucia was a perfect wife for her Anthony and returned to Chicago determined to make a match between us. Again, I resisted."

Forsythe's eyes moved over the painted face of Funicelli's wife. "Age?"

35

"Frankly, I thought Mother had lost her mind. At the time, Lucia was fifteen and a half. A mere child."

So, Forsythe thought, that would make the girl around eighteen now. Still a mere child. "Your resistance broke down?"

"Mama Rosa is a hard lady to resist. She kept at me until I agreed to go to Saffrona and look the girl over. And I only did that to shut mother up. So, I went to Sicily . . ." Taking a deep breath, Funicelli swung his chair around again. He stared up at the painting. "There she was, exactly as she's pictured. Purple-black hair, skin like satin, the face of an innocent child, the lush body of a woman. Standing by the village well, wearing a gown much like that one . . ."

The barrister studied the girl in the painting. All he saw was a fresh-faced girl, pretty and young, but that was all. "You fell in love?"

"The Sicilians have a word for it. They call it 'the thunderbolt.' An apt term. It was much like being struck over the head with a twenty-pound mallet. And this wasn't infatuation. It was a feeling that would last for life. I *had* to have her."

"You married immediately?"

"No." Funicelli gave a husky chuckle and swung back to face his guest. "If I'd had my way, I would have arranged for a priest on the spot, but her father wouldn't hear of it. He'd been hoping his daughter would enter a holy order, devote her life to the Church. Mama Rosa and I argued until we were hoarse, and finally he made a concession. We were to wait for a year and during that time, Mama Rosa would be allowed to visit Lucia, but I wasn't to see the girl. During that time, if either Lucia or I changed our minds, there would be no marriage. I was forced to agree. Robert, that year was pure hell. Half the time, I was in a daze, could hardly even attend to business.

"I came to England, found the Dower House, and brought in a construction crew to fix it up for Lucia. A year to the day when I'd seen her by the village well, Lucia became my wife. I brought her to England immediately." He passed a hand over his eyes. "I still can't believe how lucky I am.

36

Lucia is everything I'm not. So pure, so innocent, so unworldly. A saint married to a sinner."

Forsythe mentally decided this hardheaded businessman had indeed been struck by a thunderbolt. He waited while Funicelli pulled himself together. The man said ruefully, "You may consider me foolish but that's the way I feel about my wife. When Lucia became pregnant, Mama Rosa was ecstatic. She dropped everything—and Mother has many interests—to come here and look after Lucia. She issued orders that Hansel and Gretchen were to join us to meet their stepmother—"

"The twins didn't attend your wedding?"

Funicelli's mouth twisted. "The twins and I have never gotten along. As soon as they could, at eighteen, they took off and I hadn't seen them until they arrived here about six weeks ago. No, that's wrong, I did catch glimpses of them when they were picketing my meat-packing—"

"*Picketing?*"

"That's another story and I've no doubt Gretchen and Hansel will be only too happy to regale you with it." Funicelli drained his glass and set it down. "The reason I've related this soap opera is to demonstrate how I feel about my wife. Without Lucia . . . I wouldn't care to go on living without her. Do you understand?"

"I think I do," Forsythe said slowly. "Your feeling for your wife is the reason you called me back after persuading me that Buffy was mistaken, that you had no problem."

"As a Holmes, can you spot that problem?"

Forsythe's brow wrinkled and he passed a long hand over his fine brown hair. "I can take a stab at it. You did have worries when Buffy Sanderson was here, but they didn't involve your wife. Now they do."

"You're quick, Robert." Funicelli picked up the envelope, slid open a drawer, brought out a slender sheaf of envelopes, and passed them across the desk. "Read them in the order they were received. This is the latest, the one I opened shortly after you left with Tip."

"Four letters," the barrister muttered. "Heavy, expensive cream stationery. Typed. Red ribbon used." He flipped open an envelope and extracted a sheet of notepaper. "The top of this sheet neatly clipped off. Mailed in"—he peered at the envelope—"in Great Whitsun." He glanced up.

"A market town about twenty miles from Safrone." Funicelli added, "The first one arrived four weeks ago. One has arrived each week. No worry about prints. I've had them checked. None but mine on the letters. Any number on the envelopes, probably from the mail handlers."

"No doubt." In turn, Forsythe read the first three letters aloud. Each consisted of one sentence. "Anthony Funicelli is a monster spawned in the deepest slime of hell. He deserves to die a foul death. Soon this demon will receive that death." He shook his head. "Sounds like a religious fanatic."

"It does."

"You received these three letters before Buffy visited your home?"

"Two of them. The third arrived the day he did. I'll admit Buffy was right. They did upset me."

"Why didn't you tell me about them when we met?"

Funicelli's powerful shoulders moved in a shrug. "This isn't the first time I've received hate mail, threats. A man in my position acquires many enemies. But there was something about those things that chilled me."

The barrister's eyes locked with Funicelli's. "More than the wording chilled you."

"Correct again. There are a couple of points . . . but read the one that just arrived."

Again, Forsythe read aloud. "And with Anthony Funicelli shall perish his scarlet whore, Lulu." He put the sheet on the desk. "As long as you alone were being threatened, you weren't going to investigate. But now your wife is a target, too. Those enemies you mentioned . . . any one who immediately comes to mind?"

"Dozens. Disgruntled employees, business rivals." The older man waved a hand. "People who have been affronted by takeovers and buyouts I've had a hand in. But you can forget them. The creature who made those threats is close to me, probably right on this estate."

"What were the couple of points you mentioned?"

"Three now." Digging into his jacket pocket, Funicelli pulled out a key ring. Selecting one, he unlocked the shallow drawer across the front of his desk. Forsythe bent forward, caught a glimpse of a pile of stationery, the deadly blue-black of a handgun, a thin metal box. He took the sheet of heavy cream-colored stationery Funicelli was extending. At the top of the sheet, richly embossed, was the name of the house and the address.

Forsythe picked up one of the threat letters and aligned it beside the unused sheet. "That explains why the tops were clipped off. Now, the second point."

Taking another sheet, Funicelli swung his chair to face the ancient typewriter. He rolled the paper in, adjusted the tape control, and rapidly, with two fingers, typed in red letters. Forsythe got to his feet, circled the desk, and looked over Funicelli's shoulder. Funicelli glanced up at him. "I've copied the fourth letter. Notice the lowercase *a*. Ah, you see it."

"There's a tiny chip out of the top of that letter. Yes, that's the machine that was used for all four letters." The barrister paced up and down the room. "The stationery came from here; your typewriter was used. . . . That fourth letter. You call your wife Lucia."

"Lulu is my pet name for her. You see, her maiden name was Lucia Luciani. But the only time I use that name is in my home."

Forsythe stopped pacing and slumped down in the chair. He rubbed at his brow and his host asked, "Another drink?" When the barrister shook his head, he added, "You look tired. Would you rather continue this later?"

"No. The chief constable is a friend of yours. Have you thought of consulting with him?"

"Not for an instant. After what I've shown you, you must understand why this must be looked into discreetly. Robert, I'm willing to pay you any amount if you—"

"Money is not important." The barrister's hand dropped away from his face. "The important part is to protect you, to protect your wife. The person who wrote those letters must have access to this house, to this room, unless . . ."

39

"Unless what?"

"These letters could have been typed at any time. That stationery, that old typewriter . . . have you had them at any other place? Say at your home in Chicago or the ranch?"

"This typewriter's been at both places. It was my father's and I prefer it to a more modern machine. I lug it around for my personal correspondence. But this notepaper . . . no. The only supply is right here."

"Locked in that drawer?"

"Some of it." Reaching for a lower drawer, Funicelli pulled it open. "I keep some in this drawer, too. The reason I lock part of it up is that my relations have a habit, if they're short of paper, of raiding my supplies."

"Hmm." The barrister templed his fingers and stared down at them. "Do you lock this room when you're not using it?"

"Never."

"So, any resident of this house could come in here, use that paper and that machine. Any of them would know your pet name for your wife. You've had no guests who might have—"

"We've had few guests. My professional life is so hectic, I value a quiet life at home. Then there's Lucia to consider. She lived in a tiny village and then, of course, spent most of her time at a convent. Thus far, our guests have been Sir Cecil, a couple of elderly friends of my mother, and Buffy Sanderson. All out of the question."

"Don't you entertain business associates?"

"I keep my private life entirely separate from my business concerns. I maintain a suite of offices in London and if entertainment is necessary, I do it in that city."

Forsythe still had his eyes fixed on his hands. Before her mother-in-law's and stepchildren's arrival, Lucia must have had only her husband, his cousin, and a few servants for company. It sounded as though it had been even more cloistered than the girl's life in Sicily. Perhaps, he mused, when the thunderbolt struck Funicelli, it had produced a husband with an avid desire to keep his child wife only for himself.

40

He tried another tack. "Tip tells me that a woman named Flower is in your employ."

"The Flower family works for me. Sir Cecil asked me to keep them on. They live at the lodge, near the gate of the estate. Flowers have been retainers of Safrones for generations. There are two sons, Jacob and Noah, and they take care of the outside work. Mrs. Flower is housekeeper and helps Tip with the cooking. They don't get on well, so they take turns: Tip cooks one day, Mrs. Flower the next."

Forsythe lifted his eyes. "Tip mentioned a daughter."

"She worked as housemaid for a time but she left months ago to live with an aunt in Scotland."

The barrister sensed that Funicelli wasn't eager to discuss the Flower daughter. He didn't press. "Are the Flowers religious people?"

His host laughed. "Understatement. They belong to some offbeat sect—"

"Offbeat?"

"They call it—" Funicelli's low brow furrowed "—I think it's called Chapel."

It was Forsythe's turn to laugh. "Hardly offbeat."

"Anyway, the Flowers don't believe in alcohol, personal adornment, any kind of pleasure." A blunt finger tapped one of the cream envelopes. "I see what you're getting at. The wording of these letters."

"And Mrs. Flower, as housekeeper, would have ready access to this room. What about her sons? Do they have reason to come into this room?"

"Once a week for their pay envelopes."

"Where is their pay kept?" In answer, Funicelli slid open the shallow drawer he'd unlocked and pointed at the flat metal box. The barrister's eyes lingered on the handgun. "It looks as though we can add Noah and Jacob to our list."

"Not Noah. Poor chap can neither read nor write. Noah had some kind of illness when he was a child and has a mental age of around five or six. Good gardener, though, and with a wonderfully happy nature. He's quite a contrast to his mother and older brother."

"Would the mother or Jacob have the education necessary

41

to compose those letters? The wording and spelling hints at an educated person.''

''I doubt either of them have much formal education, Robert, but they're well spoken and Sir Cecil mentioned both of them are avid readers. Yes, I imagine either Mrs. Flower or Jacob could compose them. You know, this line of reasoning comes as a relief.''

Forsythe had no doubt it did. Considering that a couple of employees were intent on murdering one would be preferable to having to face the fact that blood kin had that urge. He cautioned, ''It's only a thought. The person who composed these letters might have deliberately tried to direct suspicion toward the Flower family. Now, about the daughter—''

''I'd prefer not to discuss that girl!''

''You have no choice. I've a feeling she could be important.''

''Can't hide anything from a Sherlock Holmes, can I? Remember that reference I made to a soap? Well, here comes another twist. Peony Flower—''

''*Peony?*''

''Mrs. Flower's notion of a pretty name. Her only weak point, as far as I can tell, is her daughter. Gave both her sons biblical names and picked her youngest child's straight from a seed catalogue. But, back to Peony. Shortly after we settled on this estate, Mrs. Flower suggested we take the girl on to help her with the housework. I agreed but, after I'd seen the girl, I had second thoughts. Her mother dressed Peony in loose dark dresses that came almost to her ankles, she wore no makeup or jewelry, but it was clear enough what the girl was. Definitely Peony was on the make for any man she could get. All the signs: getting into positions where she showed a lot of leg, brushing against you when there was no need, managing to touch your hand when she gave you a cup or plate. In her mother's language, I'd call her a Delilah. I considered discharging Peony but decided against it. I should have followed my instincts. She managed to raise hell.''

''How?''

''The reason she's been sent away is that she's pregnant.

And you know who she claimed the father was?'' Funicelli flushed hotly and raced on. ''Me!''

''How old is she?''

''About sixteen, maybe seventeen. I don't really know. But she was just out of school when we arrived here. Anyway—''

''Did Peony Flower definitely accuse you?''

''Not in so many words. But she must have hinted to her family that I was the man responsible. The Flowers were in an uproar. Jacob swore he'd be taking the matter up with the police for, as he put it, 'interfering with a minor.' I told him to do that and not only would he and his family be discharged but I'd see they never get another job. That cooled him down in a hurry.'' Funicelli smiled and there was a hint of cruel satisfaction in that smile. ''I told them the truth. That I'd never liked the girl and certainly hadn't seduced her. I said that probably she'd gotten in trouble with one of the village louts and was afraid of owning up. It ended up with me giving them a sum of money and ordering them to get that girl off my property.''

''Wasn't paying them off an open admission of guilt?''

''Certainly not! It was simply a gesture of charity. Mother says I think money will buy anything and maybe she's right. But, at times, it does work.''

Forsythe shifted and dug out his pipe and tobacco pouch. He stuffed dark fragrant grains into the carved bowl. ''Why didn't you get rid of the whole lot?''

''I'd promised Sir Cecil to keep them on. He told me something about their family history. Flowers have been born, lived, and often died in the lodge. They seem to be rather an inbred bunch, have a tendency to intermarry. Mrs. Flower and her husband were first cousins. I was forced to keep my promise but I did hope they might be irate enough to quit. No such luck. But they did send away that loose little slut and things have been a bit strained but fairly peaceful since.''

The barrister finished loading his pipe and touched a match to it. When he had it going nicely, he noticed his host had opened the ebony box and was clipping a cigar with a tiny

43

gold instrument shaped like a guillotine. The other man's hands were covered with dark hair that curled down over the back of them in a thick mat. Powerful hands, powerful body. Powerful in all ways. The Flowers would be no match for a man like this. Funicelli could crush them like ants. "It would appear the Flower family have good reason to hate you," Robert muttered.

"An excellent motive." Funicelli touched flame to his cigar and the rich aroma of a Havana drifted across the desk. "Better concentrate on them."

"I'll certainly look into it, but it might be one of your relations."

"I doubt it, but do things your way."

Thanks a heap, Forsythe said silently, I fully intend to do just that. His knee, injured in his school days, was aching, and he rubbed it as he said, "What security do you have on this house? I didn't notice anyone patrolling the grounds."

"I didn't think guards necessary. Not in a quiet place like this." Funicelli took a puff on his cigar. "I had an excellent burglar alarm installed, but it is only turned on when I'm away. When I'm here, I don't bother."

"How often are you away?"

"Frequently. I have to go to my office in London and occasionally to New York or Chicago. I try to make my absences as brief as possible. Sometimes I leave for a few days, sometimes a couple of weeks. But my wife, and now my mother, are never left alone without a man on the premises. Fredo has a cottage on the grounds and he moves into the house when I'm not here. Tip, of course, is always here. The exterior doors are kept locked and that seemed to be all that was necessary."

"Do the Flowers have keys to the house?"

"Mrs. Flower does, so Jacob, of course, would have ready access to them."

"That handgun in your drawer," the barrister said, "did you get that after these letters started to arrive?"

The older man gave his rich chuckle. "Hardly. That handgun happens to be a Smith & Wesson thirty-eight. It belonged to my father. Father insisted every Funicelli,

44

regardless of age or sex, know how to handle a gun. We're all good shots, but my mother, oddly enough, is our champion. A regular Annie Oakley.''

"Are there other weapons in this house?"

"Tip has a twin to my thirty-eight and Mama Rosa has a derringer Father gave her. Fredo has a revolver in his cottage. The twins? I've no idea but I'm inclined to doubt it."

Forsythe glanced at his watch. "We'd better wind this up."

"Yes, you'll want to freshen up before dinner."

"Have I permission to speak with the members of your household?"

"All of them except my wife. I don't want Lucia disturbed. And do keep in mind none of them know anything about these letters. You may find it hard to get the Flowers to talk."

Knocking out his pipe, Forsythe rose. "There's always a way to get people talking."

"You're an expert at that, aren't you?"

"I've certainly had lots of practice." Forsythe exited the room. His knee had stiffened and he was limping. He paid little attention to the discomfort. He was busy tabulating the number of people on this estate who might have reason to hate Anthony Funicelli. There were still some to meet, but right along with the Flower family, he listed the names of Funicelli's children and his Mexican houseman.

CHAPTER FIVE

ANTHONY FUNICELLI'S DINNER WAS A BARBECUE SERVED in the tropical courtyard. Additions to the area had been made—an elaborate gas barbecue, a scoured worktable, a white iron table that could easily have seated twelve. Only half that number took places there, while their host, draped in an apron over shorts and a T-shirt, presided at the grill and issued orders to his houseman, who was chopping vegetables at the worktable.

Drinks had been provided, but the only alcoholic ones were being consumed by Forsythe and Fredo Clemenza. Fredo clasped a tall beaded glass of bourbon and the barrister contentedly applied himself to a mellow Scotch. He had taken Funicelli's advice and was wearing thin cotton pants, a short-sleeved shirt, and the leather sandals he used in lieu of slippers. He decided the twins' remark about the courtyard was correct. This place, particularly at night, was indeed pleasant. Darkness crowded against the glass roof and the area was not overpoweringly lit. Strings of fairy lights were looped through the palms and a few old-fashioned light standards provided an interesting pattern of light and shadow. The odors were pleasant, too. The perfume of blooms and the tantalizing smell of cooking meat tickled his nostrils.

Sliding back comfortably in his chair, he allowed his eyes to wander around the table. At one end of it, the twins were perched with a wicker basket between them. Apparently, they were picnicking and had brought their own supplies. They were now well covered, wearing identical outfits of black leotards and loose silk shirts. Gretchen wore small gold hoops in both her ears, her brother wore only one. They were sipping a pale orange concoction poured from their thermos.

Across the table from the barrister was Funicelli's saintly wife, flanked by Fredo and Mama Rosa. Lucia's lustrous hair, pulled into a crown of curls, was indeed purple-black and a cream dress bared her shoulders and drifted around a body that looked heavier than it had in the oil painting. Her low-cut dress displayed an enticing cleavage and every time she moved, large and shapely breasts surged against cream material. Lucia didn't really look like a saint, Forsythe thought, but she was truly a luscious morsel.

Lucia moved, extending her glass, and her breasts surged again. "Tip, please give me another drink. And not this diet stuff. I don't like it."

Tip took the glass and looked at Mama Rosa. "Diet soft drink," that lady said firmly. As firmly, she told her daughter-in-law, "No arguing. You know what Dr. Fish told us."

The girl's ripe pouting lips pouted even more. "Anthony, I'm dying from hunger. I want *big*, big meat."

Her husband gave her an adoring look. "Darling, Mama Rosa picked out your steak. You must listen to your doctor and Mother."

She tossed purple-black curls and glanced across the table. "Robert, they are so *cruel* to me. Pregnant women always gain weight. Why, there was a girl in Saffrona who weighed two hundred pounds when her baby was born and she had no trouble at all giving birth."

"And that's exactly what you'll weigh if you don't listen to reason," Mama Rosa told her tartly.

The girl sighed. "I must starve another six months. Anthony—"

"Coming right up, angel. Done just as you like it." Funicelli flipped steaks onto two plates and carried them over to the dining table. He set one down in front of Mama Rosa and put the other in front of his wife, managing to brush his lips over her curls. "Doesn't my little Lulu speak excellent English, Robert? She learned it in her school and it makes it much easier for me. My Italian's rather rusty."

Lucia said primly, "The good nun who taught us English was an American who once lived in New York."

Forsythe could believe that. The girl's accent was definitely an American one.

Tip set down two bowls of salad, one large, the other smaller. Eagerly, Lucia reached for the larger helping and Mama Rosa touched Tip's white-clad arm. "Did you use the diet dressing?"

"Si, Señora Rosa, always I use the special food for Señora Lucia."

Lucia lifted imploring eyes to his swarthy face. "Will you make me one of your nice dinners tomorrow night, Tip? You always cook something I'm allowed to have huge servings of."

"Alas, señora, tomorrow night the good Mrs. Flower cooks. But the night after . . . si! I shall cook a dinner for you in honor of your fine doctor."

"Fish! Wonderful! I can have all of that I wish, can't I, Mama Rosa?"

"So long as the sauces aren't rich. Tip, remember that."

"Señora, I promise the sauces will not be rich."

"Tip," Funicelli called sharply. "Get over here and lend a hand. I'm ready for more steaks."

Before he scurried back to his master, Tip managed a sly wink at Forsythe. Fredo had left the table and was making his way, glass in hand, toward the bar. Forsythe noticed he tipped as generous an amount of bourbon into the glass as he had the first time. Taking a drink, Fredo wandered over to his cousin, spoke to him, and poured coffee from an insulated jug into a pottery mug. He set it down beside the barbecue. The two men were again wearing almost identical clothes. Funicelli's shorts were black, Clemenza's navy blue, but that was the only difference. From this distance, they looked like twins.

The barrister had forgotten all about Hansel and Gretchen

but apparently Mama Rosa hadn't. Putting down her fork, she said. "What is that revolting mess you two are gulping?"

The twins were working on bowls of green stuff that looked remarkably like a number of caterpillars squashed into pulp. "Not gulping, Mama Rosa, savoring," Gretchen said demurely. "And it's a healthy diet. Pureed spinach, avocado, and celery." She turned her flaxen head. "How do you like your steak, Lucia?"

"Delicious."

Hansel grinned. "When Father takes you to Chicago, you must have him give you a tour through his meat-packing plant and show you the humane way—"

"Hansel," Funicelli roared. "That will be *enough*!"

"I'm only trying to entertain our new mother," Hansel told him. "As a matter of interest, Lucia—"

"That *is* quite enough," Mama Rosa said softly.

The quiet remark did what Funicelli's bellow hadn't. Hansel applied himself diligently to his meal. Finishing the last scrap of meat, Lucia again gazed at the barrister. "Some English words I do not know yet. What does this 'humane' mean?"

Forsythe had no chance to reply. Gretchen, a devilish light in her eyes, murmured, "A quality of compassion, tenderness, mercy."

"Ah, this is my Anthony." Lucia chirped, "Anthony, you are *my* humane."

Her humane made no response. He bent his head, lifting sizzling steak to platters. With Tip at his heels, Funicelli carried the platters to the table. Forsythe gazed down at his serving. The steak was enormous. Covetous eyes fixed on this bounty, Lucia was again speaking to him. "I did so enjoy meeting your nephew, Buffy—"

"My secretary's nephew."

"Such a nice boy. Buffy told me he comes from a family with nine children. My Anthony and I are going to have many children, perhaps nine, too."

Funicelli, looking as though another thunderbolt had struck him, lowered the other platter in the place where his cousin had been sitting. "Let's not be greedy, Lulu. One is quite enough. After all, we must have time for ourselves."

"I love little babies," Lucia said firmly. "We are going to have a large family. This time I will give you a son, the next time I shall hope for a girl."

Tip was offering the barrister a bowl of salad and a plate of hot rolls. He also managed, when his back was turned to the other diners, to give Forsythe another wicked wink. Funicelli, who didn't like children and had just been promised a litter, took his feelings out on his cousin. "Fredo," he snarled, "get over here before your meat cools."

Fredo had returned to the bar. "You have it. I'm not hungry."

His cousin glared at him, then shrugged, and slid down beside Lucia. She gave him a radiant smile and nudged his arm. "Give Lulu a taste of your steak."

Cutting a sliver from the huge steak, her doting husband forked it into her greedy mouth. It was his mother's turn to shrug. Opening a silver case, she took out a cigarette. Forsythe extended his lighter. He admitted his introduction to the Funicelli matriarch had been a shock. From her name, he'd built up a mental picture of a short, broad, motherly woman possibly bending over a steaming pot of pasta. Mama Rosa proved to be the tallest of the family, half a head taller than her son and her nephew, with a graceful willowy body and a regal carriage. Her face, like the twins', was heart-shaped and dominated by the magnificent dark Funicelli eyes. Her skin was flawless and showed expert attention and discreet makeup. Above that lovely face was a mass of upswept hair, pure white and as fine as silken strands. In her youth, she must have been wonderfully beautiful, Forsythe mused, and if he was struck by a thunderbolt, this type of woman would be the cause.

Lucia was now caressing her husband's arm. Whether this was inspired by affection or a desire for more of his dinner, Forsythe couldn't tell. She asked sweetly, "Have you thought of a name for our son yet, Anthony?"

"There's no rush, darling."

"I have. For your father and you. Luca Anthony Funicelli. Is that not a good-sounding name, Robert?"

"It certainly has a ring. But you seem sure it will be a boy. Have you had one of those scans done?"

Mama Rosa shook her regal head. "Much too dangerous, Mr. Forsythe. But we *know* it's a boy. Don't we, Lucia?"

"Oh, yes. We tried the ancient test." The girl extended a chubby hand and wriggled the finger on which she wore a heavy gold band. "You put your wedding ring on a thread and hold it over your stomach. If it swings one way it's a girl, the other it's a boy. All the old women in Saffrona swore the ring never lied."

Forsythe smiled and touched the ring with a fingertip. "That's a handsome wedding band."

"My Anthony had it made especially for me in Mexico City. He had this made at the same time, as a wedding gift." Lucia tugged at a fine gold chain and pulled an object from the depths of her décolletage. "Is this not nice?"

Lucia was bending over the table, giving Forsythe a bird's-eye view of heavy white breasts. This young woman was certainly lavishly built. Wrenching his eyes from that view, he held out a palm and she slid a gold crucifix onto it. Her fingers, warm and soft, touched his hand, but the metal, fresh from its snug nest, was even warmer. "What splendid workmanship," he marveled. "Anthony, this was made in Mexico City?"

"I'd heard of a famous goldsmith there and I wanted something exceptional, so I had him make up the ring and the crucifix. He's quite old and temperamental but the man is an artist."

Lucia slid the pendant back down her dress. "I treasure this, Robert. That is why I wear it next to my heart. Anthony suffered so horribly to get it for me."

Funicelli said casually, "Don't make a big thing of it. Simply a touch of gastroenteritis—"

"More than a touch," his mother said. "He was hospitalized for several days, Robert, and had to wire for Tip to go down and take him back to the ranch to convalesce." She turned her head toward the barrister. "We were on pins and

51

needles that Anthony wouldn't be able to get to the wedding. When he did arrive in Saffrona, he made light of his illness, but then my son is a stoic and hates to admit to ill health. And, all his life, Anthony has enjoyed marvelous health. That was the only time he's seen a physician in years and—"

"No, Mama Rosa," her daughter-in-law said firmly. "Anthony went to London to see his doctor a couple of weeks before you arrived here. Anthony, why don't you go to my doctor in Great Whitsun? Dr. Fish is so nice."

Mama Rosa said impatiently, "My dear, your doctor is an obstetrician. Anthony, why didn't you tell me about this?"

"I knew you'd fuss. And it certainly was nothing serious."

"It's your blood pressure, isn't it? Hypertension. I've told you and told you to lose weight and get some exercise. Look at Fredo. He does a great deal of walking and—"

"I am looking at Fredo, Mother, and he's drinking his dinner. Get over here, Fredo, and have some salad at least."

If this was an effort to divert his mother, it didn't work. As Fredo wandered back toward the table, Mama Rosa bent around her daughter-in-law and looked sternly at Funicelli. "I know you keep on using that silly lift as though one flight of stairs will exhaust you. Did your physician advise exercise?"

"The reverse." Funicelli gave his mother a reassuring smile. "Calm down. My blood pressure's normal. I merely had a touch of bursitis and that's fine now, too."

To Forsythe's surprise, not only had he managed to devour the thick slab of beef but also a generous helping of salad and two rolls. His host had cleaned his plate, too, and settled back, attending to a cigar. At the far end of the table, the twins were extracting fruit from their basket and Hansel began to peel a pear. Beside the boy, Fredo gingerly picked at a plate of salad. One of Lucia's chubby hands was creeping across the table toward the last roll. Negligently, Mama Rosa brushed that hand aside and she said dryly, "Anthony, you really should have Tip build you a meal around *your* doctor's name."

52

Funicelli touched flame to his cigar and chuckled. "Now that might prove too much even for Tip's inventive mind."

Lucia clapped her hands together. "What a wonderful idea! What is your doctor's name?"

"Angus Gorinmeister."

Her dark eyes widened and she appealed to the houseman. "Tip?"

"Angus Gorinmeister," he repeated. He shook his head. "Most difficult, Señora Lucia. All I can suggest is haggis as an appetizer and perhaps Wiener schnitzel for the entrée."

Mama Rosa shuddered. "Don't bother, Tip. I think I'd rather eat one of the twins' loathesome purees."

Hansel dropped the pear core. "Don't knock it until you try it." He stretched. "Time for bed. You're in our wing, Robert. If you're ready to turn in, we'll walk up with you."

"I am a bit tired. Yes, I'll say good night now." Forsythe pushed back his chair. "Anthony, the steak was excellent. I'll see you in the morning."

"I'm afraid not. I'm driving Mama Rosa and Lucia to Great Whitsun for early mass and we'll lunch there. Lucia must see her Dr. Fish in the afternoon."

"I didn't know you were coming." Lucia dimpled up at her husband. "Tip always drives us because you're too busy."

Funicelli met the barrister's eyes. "From now on, I'm *making* the time to escort my lovely ladies."

Forsythe followed his host's thoughts. Until the identity of the writer of those letters was discovered, Funicelli was taking no chances with his wife's safety. His mother's arched brows drew together, but all she said was, "That will be pleasant, Anthony. Mr. Forsythe, you do look tired and I noticed earlier you were limping. Have you been injured?"

"An old knee injury dating back to prep school days. But, a few months ago, I was foolish enough to try skiing and broke a bone in my ankle. The cast must have put too much strain on my knee and since then it's been even more bothersome."

"Have you thought of having an operation?"

"My physician is urging that. Perhaps when time allows."

With a graceful movement, Mama Rosa got to her feet.

53

"I'm sorry the three of us will be away tomorrow, but Fredo and the twins can entertain you."

"Absolutely," Fredo said heartily. "Drop by my cottage in the morning and I'll show you around the estate. If your knee doesn't permit that, we can sit by the fire and chat."

The twins circled the table and Gretchen took Forsythe's arm. "When you've had enough chatting with Fredo, do come up and lunch with us. We'll cook something mouthwatering."

Mama Rosa made a sound much like an "ugh" and Lucia called after them, "Gretchen, that place in Chicago you said my Anthony should show me. A meat-packing concern—"

"Have your humane show you the pigsticking—"

"Shut up!" their father shouted.

As they stepped into the house, the twins were giggling. "You brats!" Forsythe said, and found he was laughing, too.

CHAPTER SIX

FORSYTHE WAS LATE IN RISING, BUT HE FOUND A WOMAN who identified herself as Mrs. Flower moving around the part of the dollhouse that passed as a breakfast room. Tip's nickname, "Dour" did seem more fitting than her real one. She was tall and gaunt, dressed in rusty black that was unrelieved by any touch of color. She had features that looked as though a sculptor had chiseled them from marble.

As the woman served breakfast, Forsythe tried to draw her into conversation. All he managed to elicit was that she had previously worked for Sir Cecil's mother, who was a "good God-fearing woman"; that yes, the house had changed since the Funicellis had bought it; and yes, the weather was damp and cold, but if the good Lord so willed it. . . . Other than that, all he gained were directions to Fredo Clemenza's cottage.

He located his Burberry, donned walking shoes, and left the house by the handsome front entrance. He walked through misty rain past the east wing and found the trail that led to his destination. He had expected a hard-surfaced road but this was a rutted lane cutting through neatly trimmed yew hedges. Keeping to the verges, where the footing was better, he limped into a dooryard. This cottage, like the gate lodge, was constructed of gray stone and capped with a weathered tile roof that might at an earlier date have been thatch.

His host must have been keeping an eye out, because at Forsythe's approach, the door swung open and Clemenza hailed him. "Filthy morning, Robert. Almost as dark as twilight already. Come in and do watch your head. For someone my height, this place is fine, but you're tall enough to get a nasty bang."

Forsythe had to bend his head to clear the lintel. The beams weren't much higher and he decided if he lived in this place, he would develop a permanent stoop. While Clemenza hung his coat, the barrister glanced around. Despite the low ceiling, he found this place more appealing than the Dower House. The furnishings were sparse but the chairs that ringed a hearth where a lively fire danced looked comfortable. He sank into one and found he had been correct. Stretching out his legs toward the heat, he said, "You didn't update this cottage."

"Hardly. I wouldn't hurt Anthony's feelings for the world, but he managed to ruin a lovely old house. He offered to remodel this cottage but I declined. We did install a bath and put some decent cooking arrangements in, but that's about it. What can I give you? Coffee, perhaps a drink?"

Forsythe glanced at the mantel clock. Ten minutes after eleven. "A bit early for alcohol, Fredo. Coffee would be fine."

Clemenza bustled into the rear of the cottage and when he returned, he set down a tray. Taking a decanter from a bureau, he put it on the tray. "Like a nip in my coffee these damp mornings. This is rather a decent cognac. Sure you won't join me?"

Shaking his head, Forsythe reached for the creamer. He noticed the other man managed to spill quite a number of nips of cognac into his own cup. Clemenza took a long swallow and smiled across at his guest. "A tour of the grounds seems to be out. How's the leg today?" When the barrister admitted it was still painful, Clemenza said, "You should really agree to an operation. Foolish to suffer unnecessarily. That's what I've always told Anthony. He fights shy of medical help, you know. Always has. When we were boys, Anthony hated it when Mama Rosa called in a doctor for some childhood ailment.''

Forsythe was looking at a framed snapshot on the mantel near the clock. Two small boys stood side by side. They were dark-haired lads with round faces. The taller one looked about six, the other was much younger. The smaller boy was clinging to the other one's hand. "You've been close to Anthony for some time?''

"All my life. My papa died before I was born and my mother was killed about ten days after my birth. Damnedest thing, Robert. Mother was taking me home from the hospital when the cab we were riding in was broadsided by a truck and Mother and the cabby were killed. I was unharmed and Uncle Luca and Mama Rosa took me in and raised me with Anthony.'' Clemenza sighed. "They were kind and Anthony is like a brother, but . . . how I wish I'd known my parents.''

"I understand. I lost my own mother when I was three years old.''

The older man was refilling their cups. In his own, he poured cognac with only a token amount of coffee. Forsythe noticed that his cheeks and nostrils were tinged with broken veins that stood out redly against his olive skin. A heavy drinker, he thought. All the signs: puffiness around the eyes, their whites webbed with red, flesh sagging along the jaw. The bloodshot eyes moved toward the barrister. "Buffy Sanderson told me about your mother's early death. Said his aunt helped your father to raise you. Miss Sanderson sounds like quite a lady.''

For a few moments, they chatted about Miss Sanderson and then Clemenza said ruefully, "I feel as though I should ask intelligent questions about the cases you two have solved, but, to tell the truth, I've no interest in crime. Now, Anthony's fascinated with crime, reads omnivorously about murder cases, both factual and fictional. And I . . . well, my interest is strictly in history.'' He waved a hand toward shelves bracketing the fireplace.

Forsythe rose and looked the books over. His host's interest was obvious. Every book on the shelves seemed to be on a historical subject. American history, English history, the history of Europe in a dozen volumes, history of the Far East, the British raj. All the books looked well handled. He took a volume down and opened it.

"If you notice one that interests you, borrow it by all means," Clemenza generously offered. "Except that one on Peru. I haven't finished it yet."

"This one on Siam, or I suppose I should say Thailand, looks interesting. I would like to read it. Thanks."

"If you'd care to lunch with me, I could make something up."

"Thanks again, Fredo, but I promised to lunch with Hansel and Gretchen."

Clemenza laughed. " 'You're a better man than I am, Gunga Din!' Lord knows what the twins will serve. At times, their humor tends to be on the macabre side. Should have seen some of the tricks the young devils have pulled on me. But basically, they're decent kids and kind of lonely and pathetic."

Forsythe carried the history book back to the circle of warmth the blazing logs provided. "I noticed that picture on top of the one bookcase. Is that their mother with them? The tall fair woman?"

"That was Ilse. She was rather pathetic, too. The twins were about six at the time that shot was taken. It must have been about a year before Mama Rosa took the children away from Ilse."

"Did their mother give them up willingly?"

"In a way. I suppose Ilse felt there was no choice. She'd managed to run through Anthony's separation settlement and she was up to her ears in debt. Mama Rosa offered her an amount for the twins that Ilse couldn't refuse."

"The children must have missed their mother."

"They did, but possibly it did Hansel and his sister no harm. Ilse never had time for them, anyway. She farmed them out to her mother and an older sister." Clemenza spilled cognac into his cup and this time didn't bother with even a token amount of coffee. "When the twins came to the family, I pretty much looked after them. I once heard Mama Rosa describe me as the Funicelli nanny. Don't get the wrong idea

58

about my aunt, Robert. Mama Rosa means well but she had little time to spare, and Anthony has even less. Of course, he's never hidden the fact that he can't stand youngsters.''

"So you were the twins' surrogate parent?''

Leaning forward, Clemenza poked the fire up. A log rolled and he lifted it into position again. Sparks fell up, giving his heavy features a ruddy tinge. "That seemed to be about all I could do. Uncle Luca trained Anthony to take over the business and he tried to train me to help my cousin. Anthony soaked it up, but I never had any talent in that direction. I do help him with his personal life, take annoying details off his shoulders.''

"Like the twins?''

"Among other things, yes. Mama Rosa picked their schools and I enrolled them and more or less kept an eye on them. Which was harder than it sounds. The little devils were always up to something and getting kicked out of school. Vacations were generally spent on the ranch and I'd be on duty there.''

"Do you live with the Funicelli family when you're in the States?''

"Whenever Anthony's in residence in the house in Chicago or at the ranch. When he's away, I have an apartment in Chicago where I stay." A touch of pride crossed Clemenza's wide face. "In many ways, my cousin depends on me. I suppose you could call me a glorified gofer. I run errands and take anything off his shoulders that I can handle. I even buy his clothes for him. His shoulders and chest are a bit heavier than mine but our legs and arms are the same length and the tailor knows exactly how to fit them on me. I've even acted as stand-in for Anthony and—''

"Stand in?'' the barrister queried.

"Comes in handy for a man like my cousin. I understand your Winston Churchill had stand-ins.''

"Mr. Churchill did, but surely you don't make yourself a target for an assassin?''

"Hardly.'' The older man chuckled, the sound reminding Forsythe of Funicelli's rich chuckle. "Invitations flood in from all over the States asking that Anthony give an address

59

at club luncheons or appear at various functions. Most of the people who issue them have never met my cousin. So, I turn up as Anthony Funicelli and let them bore me.'' He shook his dark head. ''Robert, I swear I've been faced with tons of rubbery chicken and creamed peas.''

The barrister smiled. ''Do you find it difficult?''

''Not usually. Short speeches are written for me to read and one of Anthony's bright young men is always with me to cope with anything I can't handle. I simply turn up, say the right things, shake hands, and generally be sociable. I rather enjoy it and it helps Anthony, you know.''

Yes, Forsythe thought, this man might indeed enjoy playing the part of his powerful cousin. ''You've never married or had a real home of your own?''

''Never had any inclination to do either. I'm quite content as I am.''

Then why are you drinking in the morning? Forsythe wondered. That hardly sounds like contentment. His host was reaching for the decanter and Forsythe rose to his feet. He had a feeling he was going to get no more from Fredo Clemenza.

''Are you leaving so soon, Robert?''

Forsythe slipped on his Burberry. ''I'm afraid I must. Can't keep the twins waiting.''

''Better brace yourself. If they do stir up something completely inedible, Mrs. Flower can fix you lunch. She's on kitchen duty today, and although her cooking is plain, it's fairly good.''

''Are Tip and the housekeeper feuding?''

''You could say that.'' Clemenza smiled. ''When it's one of their turns to cook, the other isn't allowed to step into the kitchen. Has to do the housework. Mrs. Flower and Tip mix about as well as oil and water. He figures she's a pain in the neck and Mrs. Flower considers him an infidel.''

''Tip seems a good houseman.''

''If he wasn't first-rate, Anthony would never keep him on. Wait a moment. You forgot the book. Here, Robert, keep it as long as you like. If you wish, take it back to London.''

''Thanks, I'll try to finish it before I leave.'' Ducking his head to clear the lintel, Forsythe stepped into the dooryard. The fine rain had turned to pelting sleet and he turned up the collar of his coat and slipped the book into a deep pocket.

"Would you like an umbrella, Robert?"

"Never use one."

"You English like walking in the rain, don't you?"

"Some may, but I don't happen to be one of them."

As the barrister reached the trail, he glanced back. Clemenza was standing in the doorway of his cottage, the coffee cup still clasped in one hand. He lifted his free hand in a wave and Forsythe waved back. What were the words Fredo Clemenza had used to describe the twins? Lonely and pathetic. He had a feeling those words also described Clemenza. It sounded as though his entire life was devoted to doing small services for his cousin.

By the time Forsythe reached the Dower House, he was drenched. Neither of the servants was in the gutted manor, and as he crossed the conversation pit to the staircase, he cast a glance at the fanciful lift. He was tempted to try it but made his way up the staircase instead. Opening the door of the upper east wing, he looked down the hall that ran its length. The walls were paneled in mahogany and recessed lighting beamed softly down. Without that lighting the hall, which ran along the outer wall of the addition and was windowless, would have been as black as midnight. The door to his room was the first of a number of doors.

Stepping into his room, he glanced around. Wide doors opened on the balcony and he could see the far side of the courtyard, the line of glass doors in the upper west wing that housed Funicelli and his bride. He slid the door back and stepped out on the balcony. Eternal summer reigned in the courtyard. Long bars of lights attached to the metal beams of the glass roof had been switched on and gleamed on the blue surface of the lagoon. Despite the inviting warmth, the courtyard appeared to be as deserted as the manor had been.

He entered his room, stripped off his damp clothes, and proceeded to dress for lunch. Taking out a pair of corduroy trousers and a light pullover, he found he was wishing he'd had time to pick up the coveted jeans and sweat shirt. While he brushed his hair, he glanced around the room. Comfortable, but as impersonal as many hotel rooms he'd stayed in. There were few personal touches. His hairbrushes were on the chest, a pile of his books were on a bed table, a leather folder beside the books. Picking up the folder, he looked wistfully down at the photograph. He'd taken this shot of Jennifer himself on the patio of her beach house at Lake Tahoe. She was wearing a white sun dress that clung to her slender body and her long hair was blowing away from her face. No thunderbolt had struck when he first saw Jennifer Dorland. In fact, love had come on slow, stealthy feet and one day he'd realized that he wanted to spend the rest of his life with this woman. Jennifer wasn't beautiful, she wasn't even pretty, but she was talented and fascinating and had a strong sense of humor. Forsythe sighed. Someday, he thought, someday. Not now. Their careers kept them apart. He didn't expect Jennifer to give hers up; she didn't expect him to, either. Stalemate, he thought, but they still had times together. Weekends, vacations stolen from busy lives. Not enough, but for now it must suffice.

Replacing the folder, he made his way down the hall to the twins' quarters. As he knocked at their door, he noticed that a spiral staircase led from the end of the hall down to the lower floor.

It was Hansel who opened the door. A paint-spattered smock partly covered his jeans and T-shirt. Over his shoulder, he called, "Gretchen, our guest is here."

"Bring him in and see if you can sucker him into buying some of that awful stuff of yours."

"Step into our lair, Robert. Notice how money-hungry my sister is? Not even over the threshold and she's trying to con you into paying for your lunch."

Forsythe's impression of their lair was size and light. Not only was there reflected light from the courtyard but daylight streamed down from numerous skylights in the vaulted ceiling. "Looks like an atelier, Hansel."

"Exactly what Father designed it for, at Mama Rosa's urging. The bait to lure us into the trap. To be truthful, it's one hell of a lot better than anything we have in our Vermont cabin. Right, Gretchen?''

"Stop making conversation and sell him something," his sister called back.

There was no sign of the girl in the huge studio. However, toward the rear, there was a partition, and she must have been behind it. She obviously wasn't cooking lunch, because the kitchen equipment was ranged along the partition.

"Gretchen's making herself beautiful for you," Hansel explained. "This is my area over here and for God's sake don't make empty compliments."

His part of the studio consisted of rows of paint tubes, stacks of canvases, two easels, and a table littered with knives, palettes, brushes. Forsythe wandered around. "You're a painter."

"Most discerning, Robert. Mama Rosa, who sponsors young artists, advises me to either take up house painting or keep on doing daubs on pottery. She's being beastly unfair. I've only had time for this sort of thing since we arrived at the Dower House. At home, I'm busy working on pottery to sell to unwary tourists at our local gift shop."

Forsythe was looking the finished canvases over. He found he agreed with Hansel's grandmother. There were a couple of still lifes of fruit and flowers, one incredibly stiff seascape, a lopsided exterior of the Dower House, and another that resembled a Technicolor nightmare. A waste of materials, Forsythe decided, and then paused. Propped against the wall was another painting and this was framed. It was much smaller than the rest and was definitely not a daub. He picked it up. The background looked like the corner of a room with gray-washed walls and white woodwork. Sprawling limply in that corner were a couple of rag dolls with yarn hair standing up around round faces, black shoe-button eyes staring—Raggedy Ann and Andy, looking as though a careless child had thrown them down. Andy's head rested against Ann's shoulder and one arm was across her aproned lap.

Forsythe frowned down at the painting. It was simple, not really expertly done, but there was something. . . . Then he saw it. Those dolls looked like the twins. The way the hair spiked up . . . those huge dark eyes. He glanced up into Hansel's huge brown eyes. "I like this. I'll make an offer on it."

"Sorry." The boy plucked the picture from the barrister's hands. "This one isn't for sale."

"Don't be an ass," his sister called. "Take the man's money."

"Your sister has excellent hearing," Forsythe commented.

"Ears like a dog's. Gretchen, Robert is talking about my doll painting."

"Oh." Gretchen stepped around the edge of the partition. Whether she had actually tried to beautify herself, the barrister had no idea, but she was dressed like her brother. "Hansel won't part with that, Robert. Says he's going to hang it over the mantel in our cabin. Come have a look at my work. You may find something that catches your fancy."

Gretchen's work area was near the kitchen and consisted of a long table covered with chunks of wood, shavings, sawdust, bottles of stain and varnish, and small sharp knives. At one end of the table, there was a set of metal shelves with knickknacks lined up along them. Gretchen picked up a small carving. "I made this for Tip as a going-away present. Think he'll like it?"

The girl was more skilled with her carving tools than her brother was with his brushes. The carving was clever, showing a tiny Mexican wearing a sombrero and a serape, and leaning lazily against a donkey. The Mexican's face was covered by the sombrero, but the donkey had a face that looked much like Tip's and one eye was closed in a parody of his wicked wink. "I'm certain Tip will like this," Forsythe said slowly. "A going-away present?"

"Us, not Tip. Hansel and I, thank God, will soon be leaving. We've done our best by Mama Rosa and Lucia and we can't stand this proximity to Father any longer. I think Hansel and I are allergic to him." She peeled off her smock. "Have a look at the other trinkets. If there's anything you like, except Tip's present, it's yours. The price is right. Consider it a gift."

Forsythe picked up a pair of bookends. "I thought you were money-hungry."

"If I was, I'd accept the more than generous allowance Father keeps pushing at us. Hansel, make yourself useful. Slice some tomatoes for the broiler and cut that loaf of bread I baked this morning." The girl swept sawdust and shavings onto the floor and laid three places at the end of her worktable. "Too bad you can't taste the bread we bake on our farm, Robert. We grind our own grain and use four kinds, as well as our honey and eggs in it. Simply yummy."

Replacing the bookends, Forsythe wandered over to the table and sat down. "What do you do when you're not returning to nature? Picket?"

"Aha!" Hansel laughed. "You've been talking to Father and he's told you what we pulled on him last fall."

"Not the details."

Gretchen was laughing, too. She poured milk into a frying pan and started to grate cheese. "He wouldn't dare talk about it. Probably send that blood pressure of his, which Mama Rosa keeps worrying about, into the stratosphere. The details are simple. We gathered up a group of like-minded people of various ages and marched en masse on the Funicelli meat-packing headquarters, waving protest placards that Hansel had lettered. Some of them were gems."

Hansel was slicing a crusty brown loaf. "My favorite was the one that read, ANTHONY FUNICELLI, THE KLAUS BARBIE OF CHICAGO."

His sister shook her dandelion head. "That was rather crass."

"To say nothing of below the belt," Forsythe muttered. "What did your protest accomplish?"

Selecting a tomato, Hansel told him, "Not a damn thing. We figured Father would be so insane with rage that he'd call the police. But the old boy was too bright for that and—"

"You *wanted* to be arrested?"

"That was our objective. Then the media would have rallied around and the world would have heard of the Funicelli son and daughter protesting the slaughter of animals. But Father kept his head and after a couple of days the weather turned foul, wind started whistling in from Lake Michigan, our fellow picketers melted away, and finally only Gretchen and I were left. The third day we had to give it up, our heads frostbitten but unbowed." He turned to his sister. "Ready for the tomatoes?"

"Stick them under the broiler. And give Robert a drink."

The drink was poured from a glass jar and was ruby red. Forsythe dubiously eyed it. "Drink up," Hansel told him. "You act as though we're trying to poison you. That happens to be pomegranate juice."

Forsythe took a cool delicious sip. "Fredo warned me about your humor."

"So, we pulled a few pranks on him when we were kids. No worry about us now. We've left childish things behind and are adults. No longer do we play jokes." Hansel added plaintively, "I'm starved, Gretchen."

"So eat," she said, and proceeded to fill plates.

The food proved to be a pleasant surprise, consisting of an excellent Welsh rarebit followed by Louisiana pecan pie. The young hosts were also entertaining. Gretchen asked demurely, "Want to hear a joke, Robert?"

"No."

"I'm going to tell it anyway. Did you hear the University of Southern Cal is thinking of switching from rats to lawyers for scientific experiments?"

"I'm now supposed to ask why. Why?"

"Three reasons. The supply is inexhaustible, there will be no public outcry, and there are some things rats *won't* do."

Throwing back his head, Forsythe roared with laughter. "See," Hansel said. "I told you he wasn't as much of a stuffed shirt as he looks."

The barrister was still smiling. "What do you brats do when you're not earning a living and picketing your father?"

Gretchen sobered and her expression darkened. "Plot revenge."

Forsythe didn't need to ask toward whom that vengeance was directed. "At the risk of sounding like a stuffed shirt, I will mention that not all fathers dote on their children."

"How many fathers kill their children's mothers?" Hansel asked. "Mama Rosa and Fredo and Father will explain that Mother's death was a tragic accident she brought on herself. Gretchen and I know better. Father is a true Sicilian. He wanted to be rid of her and knew exactly the right button to push."

Come in obliquely, Forsythe thought. Pulling out his pipe, he started to fill it. He said softly, "I saw a photo of you and your mother at Fredo's cottage. She was a fine-looking woman."

"She was," Gretchen said. "We always thought of her as a Valkyrie. Tall and blond and beautiful. We don't delude ourselves. Mother was no more perfect than our father is. The difference is that she *loved* us. Even though we only saw her occasionally, we always knew she was there. We don't blame her for taking the money and sending us to the Funicellis. Mother lived in the fast lane; she had to have money. And, even then, she came to see us. That's why she was on the ranch; that's why she died."

Striking a match, Forsythe held it well down in the pipe bowl. "How did she die?"

"Horribly," Hansel muttered. "Gretchen and I saw her die. She was thrown from a horse and trampled to death. Ironic part was that the brute was named Cupid. Mother was a fine horsewoman and was proud of that riding ability. And that's exactly what Father counted on."

"He urged her to ride the horse?" Forsythe asked.

"He *forbade* her to ride Cupid. Told her she could take any other mount in the stable but to leave Cupid alone. He said the horse would have to be destroyed because he sensed it was a potential killer."

"I fail to see . . ."

Gretchen was gazing sadly off into space. "Father pressed the right button. Mother was an obstinate woman. If she was told she couldn't do something, she immediately did it. She accepted it as a challenge."

The poor ruddy kids, the barrister thought, watching a renegade horse trample a beloved mother to pulp, obsessed with the conviction their father had caused that death—he couldn't probe those wounds further. "Fredo tells me he was called your nanny."

"So he was." Hansel's set features relaxed. "And he was a pretty fair one. Trying to please his idol—"

"Don't knock Fredo," his sister said sharply. "He was trying to do his best for us, too. Remember when you were in the hospital?" Her brother nodded his flaxen head, and Gretchen turned to their guest. "That was only a few months after Mother . . . anyway, when they loaded Hansel into the ambulance, I was certain he was going to die, too, and my brother was all I had left. Fredo was wonderful! He explained Hansel had only appendicitis and he wasn't going to die. When Fredo realized I didn't believe him, he took me right into the recovery room, pushed his way right past the nurses, and had me touch Hansel to prove he was alive. Then he arranged for a room for me near Hansel so I could be close to him and see him. Robert, we owe a lot to Fredo. As children, he made life bearable. Except for Mother and Fredo . . . well, no one else ever gave a damn about us."

Knocking his pipe out, Forsythe asked, "Not your grandmother?"

"Mama Rosa's okay," Hansel said quickly. "But she's too busy making up for wasted years to care much for anyone else. Right, Gretchen?"

Gretchen agreed and the barrister asked another question. "Then why was your grandmother so determined to take you from your mother?"

The girl said slowly, "Because we were Funicellis. Mama Rosa has a strong sense of family."

Forsythe nodded and shortly afterward took his leave of the twins. He tried to put them out of his mind. However, after a plain but well-cooked dinner provided by the dour Mrs. Flower, and an evening spent chatting with Anthony and Fredo and Mama Rosa, he found the twins were still in his thoughts. He stretched out in bed, took a lingering look

68

at Jennifer's smiling face, and switched off the light. When he closed his eyes, he didn't see that face. He saw two rag dolls with black button eyes, flaxen spikes of hair, and an aura of grief, desolation, and desertion.

CHAPTER SEVEN

The following morning, Felipe Manuel Jesus Delcardo was presiding over the dollhouse breakfast room. As he served the barrister a solitary breakfast, Forsythe asked, "Where's Mrs. Flower this morning? Tidying up one of the wings?"

"No." Tip set down the coffeepot. "Today the work load is all on this peon's shoulders. Mrs. Dour is probably pedaling her rusty old bike off to replenish her own larder. This is the dear lady's day off."

And the nearest place to shop would be Safrone, Forsythe decided. "She shops in the village?"

"Yes, indeed. A sinful morning in that riotous place. Why the interest? Do you nourish a secret passion for the lady?"

"I could work up a passion for that roast lamb she served last evening. How far did you say that village is from here?"

"Around five miles. Thinking of hiking in?"

"Hardly." Forsythe spread bramble jelly on toast. "Is there a car I can borrow?"

"The Jaguar and the Mercedes are in use. You'll have to rough it and take the minivan I use to bring in supplies. Think you can cope?"

"If you hand over the keys, I'll have a stab at it."

Tip extracted a ring of keys and worked one off. Handing it to the barrister, he asked, "Going to do some shopping?"

"I'd like to pick up something for my secretary. Any likely shops in Safrone?"

"All there is is a church, a huddle of council houses, a fairly decent pub, and a general store. And I do mean general. Sells everything from groceries to jeans. Safrone doesn't run to a supermarket. Might better try Great Whitsun."

"No gift shops?"

Tip was clearing the buffet, piling dishes on a long tray. "They have some trinkets in a corner of the general store. Pretty shoddy stuff. From what Buford Sanderson said about his aunt, I can hardly see Miss Sanderson bubbling with joy at their wares."

Forsythe drained his cup and stood up. "You haven't met Sandy." He started toward the staircase and then paused. "You mentioned the store sells jeans. Do they happen to have sweat shirts and T-shirts, too?"

"I suppose they do. Why?"

"That secret passion you mentioned. Mine is to own an outfit of jeans and a suitable top."

For a moment the Mexican looked stunned. Then, as his brilliant eyes wandered over Forsythe's elegant tweed-clad frame, he flashed his white grin. "I'd give it a pass, amigo."

Forsythe bristled. "Look, Tip, I've seen people twice my age wearing jeans."

"It isn't a matter of age, Mr. Forsythe. On you, that outfit would look as though you're planning to attend a fancy-dress party."

Feeling slightly disgruntled, the barrister went his way. He piloted the van along the narrow road leading to the village. For a change, the weather was clear, although far from balmy, and it seemed to be losing some of the chill of the past few weeks. The hedgerows showed thickening buds and beyond them, Jersey cows placidly munched at pasture. Then pastures and cattle and hedgerows fell behind and Robert slowed the van as he entered Safrone. There was a single street and he passed the church, the inn, and a tea shop before pulling the van into a parking spot in front of the general store. As he climbed down, he noticed an old bicycle propped against the steps of the store. No doubt this belonged to Mrs. Flower. Now, to hunt down his prey and engage her in conversation.

As he swung the door open, a bell tinkled over his head. He glanced around casually. Ah yes, there was the housekeeper, a wicker basket over one arm, making her way along an aisle of canned goods. Over her black dress, she now wore a shabby black coat and on her gray head perched an equally shabby black hat. Here was one female who definitely felt no need for color or adornment. Forsythe waited until she turned, caught her steely eyes, and wished her a good morning. She responded with a jerk of the black hat.

Turning away from Mrs. Flower, he approached the counter. The clerk was a fat woman wearing a bright ruffled dress and a great deal of cheap jewelry. He recognized Ruthie, aunt of Davy Crockett, alias Ronnie the straight shooter.

"Good morning," he said.

She raised her head and recognition flashed across the florid face. "Why if it isn't the gentleman who helped my sister with the kids at the station. I told Carrie, that was a kind thing to do. Not many people take time for that sort of thing these days."

"How are you making out with Ronnie and the little girl?"

"Sally's no problem but that Ronnie is a real scamp." She smiled widely. "My hubby can't abide the boy. Every time Carrie brings the boy to visit, my George swears he's leaving home. Just last night, Ronnie laid in wait for George and got him with those water guns. George was fit to be tied and Carrie took those guns away from the kid. What can I do for you, sir? Something I can help you with?"

Forsythe had noticed that Mrs. Flower, while she had no interest in personal adornment, did have her share of curiosity and had been quite motionless, clasping a can of peas, drinking in every word. He waved a hand. "I understand you have souvenirs in your gift shop."

"We don't run to a gift shop but there's some things at the end of that aisle you can look at. George just got done unpacking the latest shipment, and they sent some cute things this time.''

Forsythe set off down the long aisle, gave Mrs. Flower a friendly smile as he brushed past her, and entered a corner of the store piled high with quite appalling pieces of glass and crockery. He wandered along a shelf, picked up a plastic cow wearing an idiotic expression, a halo, and a tutu, and hastily put it back. Behind him, he heard a rustle and his elbow was nudged by a basket.

"Couldn't help but overhear, Mr. Forsythe. You're looking for a gift?" Mrs. Flower asked in a low voice.

"For my secretary. I generally take something back for Miss Sanderson." He flung out a helpless hand. "There are so many things here, I'm at a loss. Can you suggest anything?"

"Maybe I can. I was watching George unpack something really nice." She lowered her voice. "Most of this stuff is trash, but look at this." She scooped up a ceramic figurine and held it out to him.

A full-length replica of Sir Winston Churchill perched on a heavy base. It was well done. Bulldog features, cigar clutched in one hand, swelling paunch belling out the waistcoat. "It looks remarkably like the old gentleman," he said.

"It does indeed." A trace of animation flashed across Mrs. Flower's stern face and her mouth softened. "We owe so much to Sir Winston. Saved us from that horde of barbarians, Mr. Forsythe. And just listen to this." She turned a knob in the base and music tinkled out. "This is a music box. Plays *There'll Always Be an England.*"

"And you think Miss Sanderson would like it?"

"Bound to." Her mouth tightened again into a straight disapproving line. "One thing I better tell you. This I don't hold with. Screw off Sir Winston's head."

"I beg your pardon? Did you say—"

"Screw the head off, Mr. Forsythe. See?"

With the famous gentleman's chunky body in one hand, the disembodied head in the other, the barrister took a deep sniff. From the neck, a rich aroma drifted. "Demon's brew," the woman hissed. "Cognac, straight from France. But Miss

Sanderson could pour that rotten stuff down the sink and fill it with something wholesome."

The barrister's mouth was now quivering as he struggled with the thought of Sandy pouring fine cognac down a sink. Remembering the replica of the Taj Mahal, he managed to ask, "Perhaps fill it with catsup?"

"Too thick. But it would make a nice container for vinegar." She looked wistfully down at it. "I'd have liked one myself but they're so pricey."

Replacing the head, Forsythe turned the object over to check the price. By George, Mrs. Flower had done him a favor! This emblem of British blood, sweat, and tears had been manufactured in Korea. It would surely supplant the dreadful Agra souvenir as the star of Sandy's TLC. "I'm indebted to you, Mrs. Flower. My secretary will be wild about this."

The housekeeper jerked her head and, clutching her basket, headed down the aisle toward the counter. Forsythe scooped up two of the music box–decanters and tagged along behind her. When he reached the front of the store, Ruthie's fat ring-covered hands were busy. She delved into the basket and pulled out a chunk of beef. "Must find it hard feeding two boys these days, Mrs. Flower. I swear meat is one awful price."

"I know, but I can't give the boys mince all the time. They work hard and they're hearty eaters."

Ringing up the meat price, Ruthie plucked out a can of creamed corn. "How do the boys make out when you're working?"

"Have to fend for themselves." Mrs. Flower snapped open her shabby handbag. "Jacob cooks for them. Mainly fries up sausage or mince and chips. On my day off, I see they get a roast and the trimmings."

Ruthie made change while the housekeeper neatly repacked her basket. Forsythe set his figurines on the counter and Ruthie raised her brows. "You want *two* of these, sir?"

"Thought I'd better have a couple. I may never see anything like them again. Do you have boxes for them?"

"Got some already boxed right under the counter. Here you are. Need a bag for them?"

"Don't bother. I'll just stick them in the van." He glanced over his shoulder. Mrs. Flower was opening the door. He picked up the boxes. "Give Ronnie my regards and tell him he thoroughly defeated General Santa Anna."

"Huh?" Apparently Aunt Ruthie wasn't as versed in American history as her nephew was. "Who is this St. Anna?"

He didn't have time to answer; he was in hot pursuit of his quarry. He found her at the foot of the steps, bending over the bicycle. He passed her, opened the van door, and shoved the boxes under the seat. Then he wandered back to Mrs. Flower. He glanced down the line of shops and his eyes fastened on the inn. He was tempted, but he could hardly invite this woman to partake of a demon ale. He spotted a sign in the tea-shop window announcing the day's special was a cream tea. Mrs. Flower was now lifting her basket into the wire carrier.

"I was wondering," he said hesitantly, "if you would like to lunch with me. That tea shop looks rather inviting."

Her eyes widened and she stared at him. Was the tea shop also out of bounds? Forsythe added, "I hate to eat alone."

"If you stay at the Dower House for long, you'll get used to it. I swear those people don't like eating together. Have trays for breakfasts and lunches in their rooms and only get together for dinner." Her eyes darted longingly toward the sign in the tea shop and then she shook her head. "Nice of you to ask me, sir, but I better get on home. Got a lot of work to do and the Lord doesn't love slackers."

Lifting the basket from the carrier, Forsythe said firmly, "At least I can give you a lift home. Your bike and basket can go in the back. The sooner you're home, the sooner you'll get that work done."

She considered and then nodded. "As long as you're through here. Thoughtful of you."

While the barrister attended to the bike and basket, Mrs. Flower climbed into the passenger seat. She sat bolt upright, both gloved hands clasping her handbag. He drove slowly, thinking of an opening. Mrs. Flower had her own questions. "Your acts are those of a good Christian, Mr. Forsythe. What church do you worship at?"

The barrister, who rarely attended church, answered readily, "The Anglican Church."

"Hmm. There're some of their practices I don't approve of but each person must follow the Lord our God in his own way. Any of your kin Chapel?"

"I haven't many living relations, but those left are all Anglicans."

"Families do narrow down. Take the Flowers. At one time, the village was full of Flowers. Now, only the boys and I are left."

What about your daughter? he asked silently. Aloud he said, "Here we are, Mrs. Flower. What a charming home you have. Any idea of its age?"

She allowed him to help her down from the van and then she opened her bag and took out a tinkling key ring. "Don't rightly know. But Flowers have lived right here for generations. Worked for the Safrone family as far back as I know. It's different since Lady Safrone, she was Sir Cecil's mother, passed on. May her soul rest in peace. A lady she was in nature as well as title and she was kind to us." She took the basket and slung it over her arm. He wondered how to get into the gate house. Then she said briskly. "If you like I'll make up lunch for us. Nothing fancy, but I got a nice piece of ham."

"That's kind of you, but I don't wish to intrude. Won't your sons be in for lunch?"

Pushing back her coat sleeve, she consulted a nickel-plated watch. "Jacob will have already made something up for them. They breakfast early and have appetites like bears. Of course, if you'd rather not . . ."

"I should much appreciate it," Forsythe said, and headed toward the door.

She unlocked the door and stepped in. "Watch your step." Stooping, she lifted a pair of rubber boots to one side. "Noah just drops his things anywhere he's standing. Neither of my boys are too neat."

76

He saw what she meant at a glance. They were in a long room that ran the length of the cottage. Evidently, it had once been two small ones, and the cooking area was at the rear. Near the front was a stone-faced fireplace, three easy chairs, and a low table. Over the chair backs, a shirt and two jackets had been tossed; the table was piled with newspapers, books, a coffee mug, and a pair of heavy gray work socks. Near the door was a litter of shoes and boots. Despite the disorder, the room was clean.

"Put your coat down anywhere," Mrs. Flower told him.

She set an example by draping her coat over a chair back and perching her hat and handbag on top of it. Throwing down his own topcoat, he followed her into the kitchen area. It was rather a primitive place and a long pine table took up most of the floor space. She motioned toward a chair and he sat down. On the table was half a loaf of bread, a couple of plates coated with the remains of bacon and eggs, dabs of jam, smears of butter.

Shaking her head, Mrs. Flower began to clear the mess away. Gazing around, Forsythe found he was glad of the untidiness. Without that, this barren room would have been unbearable. There was no television, no radio, no ornaments, and the only wall decoration consisted of a couple of gloomy religious pictures and a photograph in an oval wooden frame. He noticed two bowls on the floor, one partly filled with water, the other with a few nuggets of what looked like dog food. At least the Flowers must have a pet. He stood up and moved over to have a closer look at the photograph. The man in it glowered back. He had fair hair, regular features, and would have been handsome if his expression had been less forbidding.

"My late husband," his hostess said. "That was taken shortly before Mr. Flower passed to his reward. I lost him young. Jacob was thirteen and Noah only ten."

And how old had Peony been? Forsythe wondered. "Fine-looking man."

She shrugged a black-clad shoulder. "God doesn't go by looks, only by deeds. Mr. Flower was a good husband and a Christian but he wasn't perfect. Only Jesus Christ our Savior was a perfect being. Rest of us just do the best we can. Take Jacob. That boy has a devil of a temper and must constantly fight it. But he does his best by his church and his family. When his father died, Jacob had to become man of the house and he was too young to take that burden on.'' She lifted the piece of beef from her basket. ''Mind if I get this ready for the oven, Mr. Forsythe? This old stove takes forever to roast meat and the boys look forward to their dinner.''

''By all means.'' Forsythe returned to the chair. ''Neither of your boys have married?''

''My Noah will never marry.'' She lifted a roaster down from a shelf. ''The Lord reached out and touched his mind. And Jacob must care for his brother. Not many young women would welcome caring for a brother-in-law who acts like a six-year-old. But Noah is happy and is as good at gardening as Jacob. Better, I sometimes think.''

''Someone mentioned that Noah had an illness when he was a child.''

''Scarlet fever, it was.'' Mrs. Flower began to swiftly peel potatoes. ''Sick that child was, you wouldn't believe. I wanted to call for a doctor, but Mr. Flower didn't believe in that sort of thing. I had both my sons in this house, with only Mr. Flower and an old aunt to deliver them. So, when Noah got sick, Mr. Flower got us down on our knees and we prayed to the good Lord to heal the boy. But Noah kept getting sicker and his little body was fair burning up. Someone told the district nurse and she came and looked at the boy and then she wrapped him up in a blanket. Mr. Flower barred her way and the nurse, and she was only a mite of a woman, looked up at him and said, 'Josiah Flower, you stand aside. If this boy doesn't get to hospital, he will die.' And she took Noah to hospital. They saved his life, but it was too late for his mind. The Lord touched him and Noah will forever be a six-year-old boy.''

Tucking potatoes around the beef, she reached for an onion. ''Mr. Flower, he never let on he felt guilt, but he must have. When he was dying, he told me, 'For this baby's birth, you are to go to hospital.' And I did. Two weeks after Mr. Flower passed on, I had my Peony—'' She stopped abruptly and put down the paring knife. "Mr. Forsythe, I shouldn't have said that name. Jacob told me, 'Mum, don't you ever say that name again.' "

"It's all right," Forsythe said gently. "I've heard the name."

Whether it was onion fumes or emotion, the barrister didn't know, but Mrs. Flower's eyes were moist. With a start, he realized that even with the drab clothes, the tightly coiled hair, and the marble features, this woman was actually handsome. As a girl, she must have been pretty. He wondered whether her daughter had those looks.

Mrs. Flower gazed past his shoulder. "Jacob says to us that Peony is dead, but hard as I struggle and pray, she can never be dead to me. She was such a bright happy little girl. Like a flower she was and that's why I named her Peony. But she was rebellious. Jacob always said we must fight the devil in her. And that devil led her into scarlet sin. But"—the woman's voice broke—"I can't believe she gave herself willingly. That monster . . . I know he took her by force."

Forsythe was reluctant to probe further. What was it Sandy had said in Maddersley? Ah, yes. "I hate what we do," Sandy had said. "We poke and pry into people's lives, we tear at old wounds, we have no mercy." A life might be at stake here, however, perhaps two lives. It had to be done. Finally, he asked, "Did your daughter accuse Mr. Funicelli of this?"

"No. As I said, the devil was in her and Peony wouldn't give a name. But Jacob said—"

"And Jacob *still* says it!"

Forsythe swung around. A man was standing behind him. The barrister saw why he hadn't heard the man's approach. Jacob had kicked off his boots and had approached noiselessly in stocking feet.

"Son," Mrs. Flower started to say.

"Who is this stranger? And by what right do you discuss this family with him?"

"Mr. Forsythe. He's staying at the Dower House. We met in the village and he gave me a ride home. I offered him lunch."

79

"He will not eat from my table." Jacob crooked a thumb over his shoulder. "Out!"

Jacob Flower looked as though he'd stepped out of the oval frame. He had his father's regular features, his straw-colored hair, his stony expression. But his eyes weren't icy; they blazed with wrath. Forsythe rose to his feet. "If I've offended you, I'm sorry, but I was only chatting with your mother about your sister—"

"I have no sister. My sister died when she was debauched by that Beelzebub at the Dower House who you call friend."

The barrister straightened his shoulders and said firmly, "Mr. Funicelli is not a friend. I met him only a couple of days ago. And I'm far from sure you have reason to slander him. You have no proof he was responsible."

"My proof is here." Jacob's finger jabbed at his chest. "And here." A finger tapped his brow. "You want proof? Very well, here is proof. For seventeen years, I've been head of this family. I have looked after the welfare of my brother and my sister as my father would have. Noah has been no problem, but from the time my sister was about eleven, she had a devil in her. She wanted sinful clothes—"

"Jacob," his mother murmured. "She was young. All she wanted was a pink cotton dress."

Her son ignored her. "She wanted paint to put on her face, ribbons for her hair, jewelry to tempt men to desire her. But I looked after her. She never set foot off this estate without either my mother or me with her. I took her to school and I brought her home again. When she went to the village, my mother was at her side. We kept her pure. But a man on this estate took her body and implanted a bastard and destroyed her immortal soul. And that man was Anthony Funicelli!"

"There are other men on this estate," the barrister pointed out.

Jacob brandished a large fist. "Which man likes young girls? Which man took a wife young enough to be a granddaughter? That man ruined my sister! Because of him, she is dead to her family, cast forth into darkness." He looked at his fist and his mouth twisted. "I, too, have a devil I must fight. I want to lash out at you, to pound this fist in your

80

face. But . . . that is sin." His arm dropped. In a husky whisper, he said, "Will you leave my house?"

Forsythe didn't argue. He picked up his coat, stepped over a pair of boots, and left the gate house. He felt fortunate that Jacob Flower had wrestled his own devil successfully. The man was his height, considerably heavier, and looked powerful. A fanatic, but a strong, well-spoken, and seemingly intelligent fanatic. The most dangerous kind.

He drove the van back to the Dower House, circled around behind it toward the converted stable that acted as garage, and spotted a kneeling figure wearing a red tartan jacket and a black leather cap working at a small but fine knot garden. This appeared to be his day for Flowers. The man had to be the young Flower son. Forsythe garaged the van, noted that although the Jaguar was still missing, a blue Mercedes was now there, and strolled back toward the knot garden. "Hello," he called.

"Hello!" The leather cap lifted. "Do I know you, mister?"

"We haven't met. I'm staying at the Dower House."

"Mommie says that place is a den of in . . . iniq . . ."

"Iniquity?"

"That's what Mommie calls it." Mild gray eyes stared dubiously from under the bill of the cap. "You don't look like a bad man."

"I'm not a bad man." A tiny dog was nuzzling at Forsythe's ankle and he bent to pat it. "Nice animal. Is he yours?"

"Jacob got him for me and said I have to look after him myself. I do, too. Give him food and water and I walk him every night. I wanted to call him Samson, but Mommie said no, that's blah . . . blas . . ."

"Blasphemous?"

"I don't know what it means. Is it a sin?"

Forsythe gazed down into candid eyes. "I suppose it might be considered sinful. What do you call your dog?"

"Blackie. Because he's black, you see. Mommie lets him sleep by my bed at night. Jacob wanted to put him outside 'cause he pees a lot, but Mommie said, 'No, Noah can take him out when he has to go.' Blackie does tricks, too. Blackie, sit up!''

The dog obediently sat up, small forepaws waving in the air. "See," Noah said proudly. "Isn't he smart?"

"A bright little fellow. Do you like gardening?"

"I like handling plants, watching them grow. They're so pretty. Mommie says God gave us plants and flowers."

"Your mother is right." Fishing in his pocket, Forsythe pulled out a plastic bag. "Would you care for a mint?"

"I like sweets." Noah covetously eyed the bag. "But Mommie says I musn't eat them, they'll rot my teeth. Peony used to give me bars of chocolate she got when she worked at the Dower House." He clapped a big hand over his mouth. "I forgot, mister! I can't say her name. Jacob says she's dead. But she's *not* dead. Peony sent me a card with puppies on it, but Jacob tore it up." The big eyes filled with tears. "I miss her. She read me stories and played games with me."

Blast and damn that despotic Jacob Flower, the barrister thought wrathfully. He patted the tartan shoulder and Noah came lithely to his feet. Tears rolled down his cheeks. "Will she come back, mister? Will I see her again?"

Forsythe had to look up into the boy's face. A gentle giant, he thought, tall and heavily built. "Of course you'll see your sister again."

"What did she do wrong, mister?"

Forsythe was at a loss for words. He could only shake his head. He turned away and Noah called, "You won't tell Jacob, will you? Don't tell him I said that name."

"That's our secret, Noah. Yours and mine and Blackie's."

"Blackie won't talk, mister." Picking up his dog, Noah hugged the little creature. "He's smart, but Blackie can't talk."

Waving a hand, Forsythe rounded the corner of the house. Inside he hung his topcoat in the closet and stepped down into the conversation pit. A log fire was blazing on the circular hearth and Fredo Clemenza was sprawled full length on a leather divan near it. He held a book in one hand, a tall glass in the other. He marked his place with a finger. "I hear you drove into the village, Robert."

"I did." The barrister glanced around. "Where is everyone?"

"Anthony went to London early this morning. I think the twins are having a swim. Mama Rosa and Lucia drove in earlier to shop in Great Whitsun. They're back now and Lucia's having a nap. Mama Rosa left word for you to come to her quarters when you returned. Know where her suite is?"

"Tip said it's in the lower east wing."

"Right." Clemenza took a long drink. "Mama Rosa's finding it deadly dull here. She's accustomed to a hectic schedule."

"How does she fill her time in the States?"

"Good works. Uncle Luca and then Anthony set up foundations, for charity and to promote the fine arts. Mama Rosa not only administers them but sits on boards and committees. She also has a wide circle of friends and has a full social life." Clemenza stretched lazily. "I've no idea where she gets the energy. She must be . . . Mama Rosa has to be close to seventy now. But she says she's making up for lost time. Uncle Luca was a real Sicilian male, you see. Believed that women are only fit for cooking, bearing children, caring for those children." He threw back his head and laughed. "Uncle Luca died when I was fifteen, but I remember how shocked his associates were when his wife took the business over and ran it capably until she figured Anthony was old enough to handle it."

Perching on the arm of a chair, Forsythe said, "I can understand their surprise. With a background like Mrs. Funicelli's, it is astonishing. She must be a remarkable woman."

"I've sometimes thought Mama Rosa is even more Sicilian than Uncle Luca was. He never tumbled that every time he instructed his son and me about his business, his meek wife's ears were not only tuned in but she was memorizing every word he said. And Mama Rosa is as much for women's lib as Uncle Luca was against it. An odd person, really. She expects her daughter-in-law to be exactly the type of wife for her son that she was forced to be for Uncle Luca."

"She does take excellent care of the girl."

"She has a good reason." Clemenza put his glass down and spread both hands. "Mama Rosa has an obsession. Another Luca, another Anthony to head the Funicelli empire. Lucia is providing her with that heir." He sat up and glanced at his watch. "Better not keep the empress waiting, Robert. Third door down the hall."

Mama Rosa opened that door. She was wearing a fuzzy white sweater and a short black skirt. She smiled up at the barrister. "How do you like my sitting room, Mr. Forsythe? It's my idea of what a sitting room in the manor might have looked like before my son indulged himself."

"I can see that and I do like it."

The room was paneled in oak, the furnishings were period and upholstered in Regency stripes, an étagère displayed a collection of delightful Staffordshire figures, and the mantelpiece was lined with Toby jugs. The glass doors were concealed under filmy cream hangings. All in all, a most restful room.

"Come over here, Mr. Forsythe. I'd like your opinion of this painting. One of my protégés did it for me. It always saddens me. Clive was barely twenty-five and died about six months after he painted it."

In a corner of the room was a stand bearing an exquisite Madonna with votive lights at her feet. Above the Madonna was a painting in a simple black frame. Forsythe fully expected it to be a rendition of the Crucifixion or the Last Supper. He couldn't figure out what portion of the Bible this was meant to represent. It looked like a section of an olive grove. In the background was what looked like a low stone wall with several figures massed behind it. They could have been either male or female and had long hair and flowing garments.

He glanced at his companion and she gave him a faint smile. "You have to work for it. Look closely."

His eyes flickered over the canvas. Then he saw it. In the left foreground was the trunk of a tree. Toward the base of that tree . . . he bent forward. Two hands embraced the trunk, no, they *gripped* the trunk, fingernails rending the bark. Slender fingers, veins and writhing tendons stark against pale flesh. *Agony.* Simple, unadulterated agony. It was as if the owner of those hands sprawled full length behind the tree, hands clearly showing the tumult in the mind.

"You've seen it," Mama Rosa said gently. "The name of that painting is *Gethsemane.* While Clive was painting it, he was contemplating suicide. Thank God, he successfully resisted that mortal sin."

"How did the artist die?"

"In torment. Clive had AIDS."

"I see."

"I believe *you* do." She touched his sleeve. "Enough of such sadness. Do come and be seated. Although I don't pretend to be an Anglophile, I do enjoy two of your customs. We shall bask in the warmth of one and I'll ring for the other. Tip does quite a creditable tea."

Taking a chair, the barrister stretched out his aching leg toward the lively fire. He was glad his hostess approved of tea. His stomach was reminding him that Jacob Flower had deprived him of lunch. Tea, carried in by Tip, proved to be disappointing. The tray was beautifully set but the contents were meager, consisting of tiny sandwiches and thinly sliced fruitcake. While Mama Rosa poured, Forsythe helped himself to a cress-filled wafer.

She handed him a steaming cup. "I shall not spar with you, Mr. Forsythe. I didn't bring you here to admire my decor or to sip tea. There is something amiss with my son. For some time, I've sensed it. Anthony has been tense and worried. As a result, I'm tense and worried. Then yesterday . . . that was the first time that Anthony has driven Lucia and me to Great Whitsun. And he positively hovered over us. Would you tell me why Anthony was so anxious to bring you to this house?"

Her eyes were not only beautiful but bright with intelligence. Reaching for a lemon slice, Robert squeezed a few drops into his cup. Then he said, "I'm not at liberty to tell you very much, Mrs. Funicelli. But I will mention this. Your instinct about your son is correct. Anthony does have a problem."

She nibbled at her lower lip. "And not one that requires your legal expertise. Anthony has countless legal advisors. That leaves the other area you're expert in. Crime." Her eyes widened. "Does this concern Anthony's wife?"

"It may. I suggest you speak with your son. That's all I can tell you."

"Speaking with Anthony would be a waste of time. If he doesn't wish me to know, nothing can force him to tell me anything. But Lucia and my grandson . . ." She straightened her shoulders. "Can I help?"

"You might be able to."

"Ask any questions you want. I'll give you total honesty."

Forsythe bent his head to hide a smile. Total honesty! No person, regardless of how well intentioned, was capable of that. "Perhaps, Mrs. Funicelli, you can tell me something about your family, your life, and your son's."

She sat back and crossed slender shapely legs. "Very well. My marriage to Luca Funicelli was arranged. He didn't come to Saffrona to select a bride but instead hired a woman experienced in arranging suitable marriages. There were several girls in my village who qualified and the competition was stiff. All the parents were eager to marry a daughter to a wealthy American. Luca's requirements for a bride were simple. The girl must be young and pretty and healthy. Finally, I was selected and my parents were delighted."

The barrister looked searchingly at her. "Were you delighted?"

"I fought that marriage with all my strength. I was in love with a boy in the village. Paulo was poor, as all of us were poor, but he was young and romantic and handsome. But I didn't prevail. Against parents, no Sicilian girl could have. So Mother and I arrived in Chicago and were met by Luca's younger sister, Anna—"

"Was that Fredo's mother?"

"Yes. Anna had a tragic life. She was widowed shortly before the birth of her son and was killed in a car accident only a few days after Fredo was born. But back to my marriage. I didn't see my bridegroom until the wedding ceremony. When I did see Luca, I was dismayed. Not only was

86

he a man in his fifties but I knew immediately the type of man he was. Macho, not unkind but wanting only a pretty young wife to bear his children, to look after his home. Until my husband died, Mr. Forsythe, I was a mere chattel.''

Forsythe took another sandwich. ''Your son appears to view your marriage as ideal.''

''My son deludes himself. My marriage was far from ideal. I became pregnant almost immediately and when I was barely seventeen gave birth to Anthony. The pregnancy was difficult and when the child was born, I nearly died. My physician insisted on an operation that prevented me from ever bearing another child. Luca was furious and felt he'd been cheated. From that moment, I meant nothing to him. All I was fit for was raising his son and caring for his house.''

''And raising his nephew.''

''Yes, that, too. When Anthony was three, Anna was killed and her infant son was handed to me to raise. I've never pretended I like Fredo. Even as a small child, he was sly and deceitful.''

''What is the relationship between Anthony and his cousin?''

She smiled slightly. ''Lopsided. Fredo adores Anthony, and my son . . . I suppose Anthony may be fond of his cousin. They were raised together, but in his heart, I believe Anthony views Fredo as I do. Simply as a burden. I've advised Anthony repeatedly to put Fredo out of our lives, but my son has a strong sense of family and refuses to do it.''

Forsythe set his cup down and reached for his pipe. He lifted a brow, and when Mama Rosa graciously nodded, he proceeded to fill it. ''Does Fredo Clemenza have a private income?''

''No. His mother dissipated her inheritance and Fredo receives an allowance from Anthony. He's proved a most expensive burden. The amount of money Anthony has spent buying his cousin out of messes is ridiculous!''

''Messes?''

Her mouth tightened. ''You've probably noticed one of his vices.''

''He's a heavy drinker.''

"Closer to an alcoholic. He is also an inveterate gambler."

"Is that all?"

She answered the question with another question. "Isn't that quite enough?"

The barrister had a hunch total honesty had just flown out of the window. He didn't press. Instead, he asked, "Could Fredo be hiding his true feelings about his cousin? Could he secretly hate or be jealous of Anthony?"

Her arched brows drew together. "I'm certainly not an authority on Fredo. Actually, I ignore him as much as possible. But I'm inclined to doubt it. Fredo is dependent on Anthony in every way. And I don't believe the man is a good enough actor to conceal feelings like that." She added abruptly, "I've told you as much as I can about Fredo."

No, you haven't, Forsythe thought. You've told me as much as you *intend* to. "Tell me about your grandchildren. I'm particularly interested in the death of their mother."

"A tragic accident, Mr. Forsythe. Do you know any of the details?"

"The twins appear to feel that their father is responsible for their mother's death."

"The silly deluded little fools! My son did his best to warn Ilse about that horse. But she was a headstrong woman and deliberately flouted those warnings. Ilse was a fool, too!"

"Deluded or not, Hansel and Gretchen consider it a reason to hate their father."

"They hated Anthony long before Ilse's death. I was the one who decided to take them away from their mother's custody, but the twins have always blamed Anthony for that decision. As for them actively trying to harm their father . . . I doubt it. Hansel and Gretchen have taken that hatred out in small, niggling ways."

"Such as picketing the meat plant?"

"Exactly."

"Now for Tip."

Her eyes widened. "What could a *servant* possibly have to do with this?"

Better tread carefully, the barrister told himself. This

woman, once a simple village girl, was now a grand dame. Obviously, she would not believe that a servant might have reason to threaten his employer. He said cautiously, "I understand that Anthony took Tip from his family when the boy was only twelve."

She smiled. "My son took pity on a bright little boy who was in a grievous, poverty-stricken situation. Anthony brought the child to the States, educated Tip, and made him an American citizen. Anthony is the boy's benefactor. As for his parents . . ." She waved a slender hand. "Anthony has been generous to them, too, and the Delcardos are very content on the ranch. Tip's mother is acting as cook, and Maria is wonderfully skilled at that. His father is partially crippled and has only light duties. Both his sisters help out in the ranch house and the youngest child, Carlos, is receiving the best of medical care."

It was the barrister's turn to raise his eyebrows. "The Delcardos are at your ranch in California?"

"Of course. Another example of my son's generosity. Anthony checked on them, found they'd spent the funds he left with them when he brought Tip north, and also that Carlos was so ill he might die. Immediately, my son arranged to bring the whole family to California."

"Are they American citizens?"

"Not as yet. But Anthony told me he intends to have that done in time and will also provide funds to set the family up in their own restaurant. As I mentioned, Maria is a marvelous cook."

Forsythe rubbed his chin. "How long have they been at the ranch?"

"I don't really recall. Let me think." After a moment, she said slowly, "I do remember they were there on Tip's birthday. Another kind gesture. What a birthday present to give a son so devoted to his parents! Now I remember—it was Tip's nineteenth birthday. They arrived over three years ago."

Robert stood up and looked down at Mama Rosa. "One final question. Anthony tells me he dislikes children. Why did he bring a twelve-year-old child back with him from Mexico?''

"That has always puzzled me." She rose gracefully. "I should imagine it was Anthony's strong sense of charity. And Tip is devoted to my son."

In a pig's eye he is! Forsythe thought inelegantly. He politely thanked his hostess for tea and stepped out into the hall. She followed him. "Remember, Mr. Forsythe, I am depending on you to shield my daughter-in-law and my son from whatever is threatening them."

Her words sounded more like an order than a plea. As the barrister swung open the heavy door leading to the main house, he glanced back. When Fredo Clemenza had called his aunt "empress," he'd been dead on target. Mama Rosa's slender body was held proudly and overhead light turned her snowy hair into a silver crown. How, he wondered, could he have pictured this regal woman as a fat grandmother stirring a pot of pasta?

CHAPTER EIGHT

Robert Forsythe had always been inordinately fond of seafood. As Sandy had once mentioned, he considered no dinner complete without two fish courses. That evening, he finally had his fill of his favorite food.

The Funicelli family gathered around the oval table in the formal dining section as Tip, resplendent in an immaculate mess jacket, proudly served his tribute to Lucia's obstetrician. Apparently, the twins didn't indulge in fish and they were served plates of shredded vegetables. They were paying more attention to their father than to their dinners. When the first course was served, Forsythe noticed Hansel nudging his sister. With ill-concealed mirth, they followed Anthony's fork as it pushed fresh shrimp around his plate. Forsythe glanced at the other diners. Fredo was paying more attention to his wine than the shrimp, Mama Rosa was eating daintily, and her daughter-in-law was positively shoving food into her ripe mouth.

Tip's next offering was broiled trout and Forsythe concentrated on this delicacy. When the third course, red snapper, was placed before him, he felt something nudging his foot and looked across the table. Gretchen grinned and jerked her head toward the end of the table. Funicelli was glowering at his portion. "Tip," he growled. "You're well aware I *hate* fish."

Gretchen said graciously, "If you like, Hansel and I will share our meals with you."

Her father cast a disgusted look at the vegetables on his children's plates and then glared up at his houseman. Tip's broad face was impassive. "Si, señor, I know you don't care for fish but this meal is in honor of Señora Lucia's doctor. I thought you would be pleased that she is pleased."

"I should have picked a doctor with a name like beef," Funicelli muttered.

Swallowing a mouthful of snapper, Lucia said, "Caro, don't be a grouch. This is the first meal in weeks where I can eat as much as I wish."

Funicelli subsided, but a few minutes later, he jumped up and threw down his napkin. The Mexican was depositing a silver platter on the table. On it, molded into a fish shape complete with fins and scales, was a quivering pink object. "This is *too* much. I am not eating salmon mousse for dessert."

Tip looked injured. "Por favor, señor, would I serve salmon for dessert?" He transferred innocent eyes to Mama Rosa. "Señora Lucia will be able to eat much of this. It is only gelatine, skimmed milk, and crushed raspberries, sweetened with honey."

Lucia clapped her hands. "Tip, you're wonderful!"

"Nada, señora," the houseman said modestly.

By the time the sweet was consumed, Funicelli's good nature was restored. Jovially, he asked his cousin, "All ready for our backgammon game?"

"Not only ready but I have a feeling tonight I'm going to win." Fredo turned his head. "Would you care to join us, Robert?"

"I've played backgammon but I don't really care for it. Chess is my game."

Funicelli smoothed a heavy lock of hair from his brow. "I haven't been much of a host, Robert. Perhaps we'd better postpone that game, Fredo."

Clemenza looked disappointed and Forsythe said quickly, "Go right ahead. I can amuse myself."

"Very well." Funicelli circled the table and dropped a kiss on his wife's bare shoulder. "Do you mind, Lulu?"

Lucia seemed more interested in her second helping of dessert than in caresses. It was Mama Rosa who said, "We're going to be busy anyway, Anthony. Lucia picked out some marvelous material today for a crib cover and we're going to start sewing it tonight. Mr. Forsythe, Lucia and I are making the entire layette."

Animation touched Lucia's face. "We've finished our son's christening gown, Anthony. You must look at it. It is beautiful."

This time, he kissed her glowing cheek. "Leave it out, angel, and I'll look at it when I come to bed. Mind you don't work too late. Remember what your doctor—"

"Rest!" Lucia snapped. "No food, no late nights. Anthony, I'm not allowed *anything* I like."

"Don't complain." Mama Rosa got to her feet. "A few more months and you'll be able to eat mounds of pasta and stay up dancing all night." She glanced at her son. "Don't worry, Anthony. We won't sew for long and I'll tuck our little mother in before I leave your wing."

By the time Forsythe had finished his coffee, he was alone. Lucia and her mother-in-law were climbing the stairs, the twins had quietly slipped away, and Fredo and his cousin were down in the conversation pit bending over a backgammon board. Then the door to the kitchen area opened and Tip began to pile dishes on a tray.

Forsythe set down his cup. "Mind if I tag along while you clean up, Tip?"

"I'd be delighted. It won't take long to straighten up. The kitchen is state of the art. I happen to like chess, too. Perhaps we can have a game."

The barrister followed the houseman into the lower west wing. The layout was identical to the wings he had already seen. There was a long windowless hall with doors lining its one side.

Tip indicated the first door. "Here's the kitchen. My room is that door just beyond."

This kitchen was truly state of the art. Stainless steel,

93

chrome, and enamel predominated. The appliances were hotel size and there was a bank of micro ovens and several marble pastry boards, as well as the dishwashing machine the Mexican was deftly loading. Tip pointed a finger at a wall. "That's my contribution. Drives the devout Mrs. Dour frantic. When the kitchen is her domain, she turns it toward the wall."

Yes, Forsythe thought, that calendar would seem Satan-inspired to Mrs. Flower. It was a Playboy edition and the March Playmate wore a seductive smile and little else. "You enjoy baiting the poor woman, Tip."

"It helps pass the time." Shoving a rack in, the houseman shut the door of the machine. "Why don't you wait in my room, Mr. Forsythe? Have a look at my little library. They say you can tell a lot about a person from his reading tastes."

The barrister glanced around the spotless kitchen. "Aren't you finished here?"

Tip was lifting cold meat and pickles from the fridge. "I've one more chore. Sustenance for my master. Cousin Fredo is no problem; his sustenance is in liquid form, but master dotes on food. Anyway, I have to atone for the fish dinner."

"Which you cooked with malice aforethought," Forsythe remarked, and returned to the hall. He opened the door of Tip's room and then stepped back. An appalling din assaulted his eardrums. Hastily, he closed the door and returned to the kitchen. Tip was cutting sandwiches. "Back so soon, counselor?"

"Your room sounds as though a massacre is taking place."

"Sorry. Forgot I'd left the stereo on. No problem. I'll switch it off."

Forsythe waited in the hall until the stereo was switched off. "What in hell was that?"

"Heavy metal. If I'd known I was entertaining, I'd have gotten some Lawrence Welk."

Forsythe smiled. "And that has the earmarks of a snide comment. That so-called music is enough to deafen one. This wing must be well soundproofed. I didn't hear anything until I opened the door."

"All the wings are soundproofed. Not only from the main

house but from other rooms in the same wing. Mr. Funicelli is nothing if not thorough." Tip moved toward the kitchen. "Be with you in a second."

The second was more like ten minutes, but Forsythe didn't mind. He put in the time having a look around the Mexican's room. A narrow bed was in one corner, flanked by night tables piled with books and magazines. Near the glass doors was a combination chest and desk with a framed photograph on it; sound components were stacked in a wire stand and bookshelves lined one wall. When Tip returned, the barrister was running a finger down the line of books.

"I see you've already started your legal studies," Forsythe said.

"Quite a collection of legal tomes, isn't it? Did you notice my other collection?"

"You appear to have one taste in common with Funicelli. Christie, Sayers, Allingham, P. D. James—"

"The best of the Brits and the best of the Yanks. The complete works of Ross Macdonald and Raymond Chandler, as well as Rex Stout and many others. I really do love a mystery. But you must have a look at the master's collection. It not only outshines my crime collection but he has some first editions. Makes my mouth water when I run a feather duster over them. I suppose you dote on mysteries, too."

"No. My secretary is the one who reads mysteries. My taste leans toward the classics and history."

Tip motioned toward an armchair. "Have a seat and I'll get the chessboard out."

Forsythe took the chair but shook his head when Tip reached for the chessboard. "Another time. This evening, I'd rather play another type of game."

The houseman unbuttoned his mess jacket and threw it on the bed. Under it, he was wearing a T-shirt with bold black letters announcing FORGET THE ALAMO!

Grinning, the barrister said, "You should have been wearing that slogan when you went up against Davy Crockett. Incidentally, I saw Aunt Ruthie in the general store today and she tells me the king of the wild frontier has lost his guns."

The Mexican slumped into a chair. "Let's skip the small

95

talk, Mr. Forsythe. Exactly what game do you have in mind? Twenty Questions?''

"Something like that. What I'd like you to do is to give me a thumbnail sketch of every person on this estate.''

"Sort of a worm's-eye view, eh? Am I allowed to ask why?''

"Put it down to simple curiosity. And, Tip, I'd like total honesty.''

"You know as well as I do that doesn't exist. But, ask away.''

"Mrs. Rosa Funicelli.''

"As I mentioned before, a matriarch. Rather a cold lady and trying to atone for years of frustration in her remaining ones. A true-blue Sicilian. Honorable, smart, utterly ruthless. She's one person I wouldn't want to cross. How am I doing?''

"Most concise.'' Forsythe dug out his pipe and tobacco pouch. "Hansel and Gretchen.''

"Not really babes in the wood. Bright and talented and not as featherheaded as they let on. Half Sicilian, so they shouldn't be underestimated.''

Forsythe bent his head, holding a series of matches in the pipe bowl. It took four tries before he had it going. "Now, the Flower family.''

"Mother Flower is the only one I've really had much contact with and I don't know that much about her. We aren't that close. You probably know as much as I do. The family is obsessively religious and lives Spartan lives. Jacob and Noah . . . I've only seen them around the grounds and occasionally when they come to the house to pick up their weekly pay from the master. I've stopped to say a few words to Noah now and then and he's a nice harmless boy. Jacob is a different type of cat, surly and with violence bubbling under his devout front. Sister Peony fell from grace and was expelled from the Flowers' Garden of Eden.''

"Yes, I've heard about that fall.'' Forsythe puffed rapidly and smoke wreathed around his head. "Do you think Anthony Funicelli is responsible for her pregnancy?''

"No.'' A buzzer sounded and the houseman cocked his

head. "That will be the master calling for sustenance." He rose and pulled on his mess jacket. He told the barrister, "Relax and enjoy. While I'm trotting around, can I get you refreshment?"

"A drink would be welcome."

"Any particular kind?"

"Surprise me."

In a short time, Tip was back. He set two frosted goblets on the table. The rims were coated with salt. "My national drink. For tourists, that is. Ever tried a margarita?"

"Many times." Forsythe had a brief flash of Jennifer and him near a hotel pool on an idyllic day in Acapulco. "Cheers are out. You can propose a proper Spanish toast."

Tip thought for a moment, and then said, *"Salud, amor, y pesetas, y el tiempo de gustarlos."*

"Translation, please."

The houseman raised his goblet. "Health, love, and money, and the time to enjoy them."

"I'll drink to that," Forsythe said, and did.

Tip took a long swallow, "Now, on to the next victim."

"Lucia Funicelli."

"Alias Lulu the fair." The Mexican's low brow furrowed. "This one is tougher. I think we tend to discount a person's capabilities because of age or appearance. The girl is young and pretty and curvaceous, but a Santa Lucia she's not. Lucia is a Sicilian and as devious as they come. Mama Rosa watches her diet like a hawk, but the girl manages to get hefty forbidden snacks, anyway. She cons both her doting husband and me into sneaking her tidbits."

"Isn't that rather dangerous for you? If Mama Rosa should tumble—"

"She'd have my scalp." Tip grinned. "But Mama Rosa will never know about it. You see, Lucia practices her country's old watchword: *Omerta.*"

Forsythe's pipe had gone out. He placed it on the table and took a salty, icy sip of his drink. "*Omerta?* Doesn't that mean silence in the face of authority, such as the police?"

Tip's grin widened. "And who has authority over Lucia? Her husband and her mother-in-law."

He drained his glass. "I suppose Fredo Clemenza is now under my microscope. Not too much to say about him. He lives in his cousin's shadow and jumps to attention if Anthony so much as moves a finger. Kind of a sad man. Dresses like his hero and even has his hair styled much the same. Rather a dull chap. If Fredo ever had any brains, they're now pickled in alcohol."

Forsythe raised his brows. "That's it?"

"Look, I'm doing my best. I'm an amateur at this game."

"Tell me about Fredo's vices."

"I've mentioned one: alcohol. He used to be a compulsive gambler, but Anthony put his foot down and, as far as I know, the only bets Fredo places now are on backgammon."

"In the past . . . did Funicelli have to fish his cousin out of messes?"

"Any number. Once Fredo reneged on a bookie and Anthony had to move fast before enforcers used a baseball bat on both Fredo's kneecaps."

Wincing, Forsythe rubbed his own aching knee. "How do you know about the gambling? Eavesdrop?"

"As much as I can. I've always tuned in on the master's conversations. Hasn't been hard, either. Mr. Funicelli regards me as a piece of furniture. But that's all I can tell you, Mr. Forsythe. I'm not a Sicilian, you know."

"Don't be so modest," Forsythe said dryly. "You're crafty and I've a hunch you're much like a sidewinder."

The Mexican's white grin flashed. "You can be snide, too."

"When the occasion calls for it. Stop dodging. Does Fredo Clemenza have another vice connected to women?"

"You win. Girls, and the younger the better."

"Seduction?"

"From what I've gathered, more like rape. Once I heard Mama Rosa telling her son that Fredo was nothing but a pervert. His cousin managed to buy Fredo out of a number of smelly affairs, but one time the Funicelli money and prestige almost didn't work. That particular girl's parents had to be subdued by threats of violence. The master rose to the occasion because he couldn't let the Funicelli honor be besmirched. But this is in the past. For a number of years, Fredo's been a well-behaved pervert.''

''Except with Peony Flower.''

It was the houseman's turn to arch his heavy brows. ''So you tumbled, too. I can see why. Rather strains the imagination to picture Anthony the Great seducing a housemaid. But don't be too hard on old Fredo. Peony was ripe for the plucking. The girl had been held down too long, and despite the godawful clothes and lack of makeup, she's a tasty wench. One of her duties was to clean up Fredo's cottage. Talk about handing a chick to a chicken hawk! I should imagine they had many a roll in the hay before Peony's family found out she had what you English call a 'bun in the oven.' ''

The barrister was frowning. ''Funicelli protected his cousin. More or less blackmailed the Flower family into submission and had the girl sent away. Why on earth didn't she tell her brother and mother the truth about who the father was?''

Tip shrugged a chunky shoulder. ''Who knows? Maybe Peony had her own code of *omerta*. Maybe Fredo slipped her a little money to keep her mouth shut. Maybe she liked him and didn't want Jacob after his hide.''

''Was Fredo punished?''

''Nearly pulverized. I just happened to hear Funicelli go after him. He told Fredo that was the last time. If he pulled anything else, he was out of the family circle for good. That would be the worst punishment Fredo could be given. He adores his cousin, lives for a nod of approval from Funicelli. For a while, Fredo slunk around like a beaten cur, but then he wormed his way back into his cousin's favor and all was serene again.''

Forsythe shifted and rubbed at his knee again. ''One final question about the Funicelli family. Can you think of any reason one of them might want to harm Lucia?''

The houseman sobered. After a moment, he shook his head. ''Absolutely not.''

''What about the twins?''

''An unqualified no. Hansel and his sister are fond of Lucia. I think they're sorry for her because she's married to their father." He drained his glass and looked intently at the barrister. "This is beginning to sound serious and my curiosity is at the boil. Just what's going on, Mr. Forsythe?"

The barrister looked searchingly at the other man. "You said all the wings are soundproofed. Is Funicelli's office soundproofed, too?"

"No. The master didn't start soundproofing until the wings were built and his office is in the original house."

"Then you know exactly what the situation is."

"Bingo!" Tip threw both arms in the air. "I'm definitely no match for you. I'm not a Clarence Darrow yet, and you certainly are. I'll confess. Yes, I had my ear pressed to the master's door while you discussed those threatening letters. I'll admit that; until I heard his wife had also been threatened, I was delighted. Mentioning little Lulu was a master stroke. Mr. Funicelli is a tough guy but he, too, has his Achille's heel, and because of that, he's running scared."

"Any idea who could have sent those letters?"

Tip shook his dark head again. "They sounded much the same way that Mrs. Dour talks, but that could be a smoke screen." He stretched. "Well, that winds it up: this humble peon's opinion of all the suspects."

"There's still one left," Forsythe said casually. "Felipe Manuel Jesus Delcardo?"

The younger man's blue eyes widened. "You expect me to analyze myself? Shouldn't you chat up another member of the family for an opinion of Tip Delcardo."

"I've a feeling that would be a waste of time. I've a hunch few people know much about Tip Delcardo."

"Point taken." He got to his feet. "I think I could use another drink. Care to join me?"

"Not for me, but you go ahead."

When the houseman returned, he found Forsythe had moved the framed photograph from the desk to the table. Putting his goblet down beside it, he said, "I see you spotted my family."

"A fine-looking group, Tip. Well dressed, well nourished. Safe and content on the Funicelli ranch. You deliberately led me to believe you hadn't seen them since you left your village with Funicelli.''

"Objection, counselor. That conclusion you jumped to yourself."

"I won't argue the point. Now, explain why Funicelli, who dislikes children, insisted on having you."

Tip's lips quivered. "If you're toying with the idea the master is a pederast, you can forget it. The only pervert in the family is Fredo. As far as sex goes, Anthony Funicelli is rigidly moralistic. The answer to your question is simple. When Mr. Funicelli and his engineer friend entered the village of Quila, every kid in the place, except me, crowded around the two men. The master handed out largesse, candy and pesos, and the kids were wild about him. I was the holdout. Stood well back and simply watched. Finally, Funicelli pushed through the mob of brats and held out a coin to me. I snatched it and ran like a rabbit. He found out where I lived and came to see me. When he realized I hated him, he became intrigued. Although he loathes children, he prides himself on the fact that they always like him."

"And you didn't?"

"Hate at first sight. And he felt it. That's why he bought me. He bartered with my family and, as I told you, I went along with him amid the rest of the luggage. Funny, even in small things, that man has to win."

"As time passed, did you pretend to like him?"

"That would have been the smart thing to do, but I'm not that good an actor. I couldn't fake it well enough to fool the master. But, as time passed, I became useful to him and he decided to hang on to me. I suppose that was my punishment for injuring his vanity."

"He did keep his promises to your parents?"

"That he did. My household duties were light and I was sent to school. When I was sixteen, he arranged U.S. citizenship for me. After that, I started to get itchy. Could hardly wait until I was nineteen and could clear out."

"Was that part of the agreement?"

"Mr. Funicelli promised me when I was nineteen, I could leave his employ if I wished."

"And yet you're still with him."

"Under duress. On my nineteenth birthday, he had a surprise present for me. We flew in his Lear jet to California and when we got to the ranch, my family was waiting. My father, Pablo, my mother, Maria, my sisters, and "—Tip bowed his head—"my little brother, Carlos. All the time I was with them, they sang Mr. Funicelli's praises. What a *wonderful* man the master was. When he brought them north, they were in dire shape. Father is partially crippled and could earn little money. The funds the master had given them for me were long exhausted. It looked as though my teenaged sisters would have to sell their bodies on the streets to feed the family. Carlos has always been frail and he was very ill. And my parents couldn't afford a doctor or even medicine for the boy."

Forsythe eyed the bowed head. "You mentioned duress?"

"Mr. Funicelli gave my family every comfort: a house of their own, employment, clothes, food, the best of medical care for Carlos. And all that can be taken from them if I don't behave. The Delcardos will be back in Mexico, penniless, my sisters prostituting themselves, my brother dying. Do you understand? My family are being held as hostages!"

"Mama Rosa led me to understand that her son intends to have them made citizens, set them up in a restaurant."

Tip's head jerked up and his expression was bleak. "This time only one promise has been given. Mr. Funicelli promised me that if I leave him, the Delcardos will go back to Mexico. They're illegal aliens and—"

"Tip, there is the amnesty program."

"And there's a much older rule. One law for the rich, one for the poor. All Mr. Funicelli has to do is tell the police that the Delcardos stole from him, perhaps that they peddle drugs, that they are undesirables. And I'm powerless to stop him."

Tip leaned his head back and closed his eyes. Moodily, Forsythe regarded the younger man. He found that broad face somehow disturbing. In repose, without the beauty of the brilliant eyes and the flashing white smile, the heavy features looked as though they had been chiseled from brown agate, implacable, brutal. The barrister said casually, "Exactly when did Anthony Funicelli give you the promise that you could leave him when you reached nineteen?"

"Shortly after I received my citizenship. The master arranged a small celebration and opened a bottle of champagne."

"At that time, did he offer you any other inducements to stay on?"

Tip's eyes snapped open. "You definitely have a talent for cross-examination, Mr. Forsythe. Yes, he offered an inducement . . . with a provision. If I left his employ with his agreement, he promised a lump sum of money: enough to pay my tuition to law school and support me while I got my degree."

Forsythe smiled. "I see."

"Just what do you see?"

Forsythe glanced at the photo of the Mexican family. "When you were telling me about finding your family at the ranch and the danger they're in, I was wondering why you didn't bolt, take them back to Mexico and look after them yourself. Surely that would have been the answer. You'd have been free of Funicelli, and your family—"

"How would I have supported them? Working in a lousy luxury hotel? Toadying to a bunch of rich Americans?" Tip made a savage gesture. "Yes señor, no señor, I'll kiss your ass, señor! To hell with that! I'm sick of coddling wealthy Americans. I want to *be* a rich American."

"Simmer down, Tip. I only asked a question." And got my answer, Forsythe thought. With this man, family came second; self-interest definitely came first. Leaning forward, the barrister picked up the photo. It was in color. In the background was a big Spanish-type house. In the foreground were five people. A woman and two girls were gathered around a boy in a wheelchair and a man sitting with one leg stiffly extended. "My father, Pablo," Tip said. "My mother is behind his chair. This girl is Liliana, the shorter one is Delores. The boy, of course, is Carlos."

Tip resembled his mother. Maria Delcardo looked quite Indian and had long black braids, coarse features, and dark brown eyes. Both Tip's sisters had their mother's features, but they were softened by the dark hair that flowed loosely to their shoulders. The man had a thin face, sensitive features, and bright blue eyes. His skin looked much fairer. The boy in the wheelchair was a younger edition of Pablo Delcardo.

"Odd," Forsythe muttered.

"What's odd?"

"Your mother's eyes are so dark and yet every one of her children have blue eyes. Most distinctive eyes."

"Like mine. I know brown eyes generally predominate, and my mother's eyes are so dark, they look black. This is an inheritance from my father's family. No matter the color of a mate's eyes, the children always have the blue Delcardo eyes."

The barrister glanced at Tip. "Just how are you useful to Funicelli? Why would he go to these lengths to hold on to you?"

"I am good at my work, you know."

"You could be replaced with someone just as efficient."

"Ah, but could he find another slave? Think how useful it is for a man in his position to have a servant who works in his house, who travels with him, who may overhear details on takeovers and buyouts, and who never dares to open his mouth."

"And is at his beck and call," Forsythe muttered.

"Exactly. Take that time I had to go to Mexico City, get him out of a hospital, bring him to the ranch, and coddle him. When I got the call, I was having a much-needed vacation, but I dropped everything and flew down. The master was in a frightful mood. He raved on about how incompetent the nurses were, what a bungling quack his doctor was. I met his doctor and he may have been a quack, but he was a jolly little fellow. Rather a coincidence about his name, Mr. Forsythe. Maybe that's why I liked him. His first name is also my father's, his surname the same as my village."

Forsythe got to his feet. "You've painted a dreadful picture of Anthony Funicelli."

"Only because the subject is dreadful. And I've put myself

104

at your mercy. One word of this to Mr. Funicelli, and my family may be sent back to Mexico.''

"Don't worry, Tip.'' Forsythe opened the door. "I may not practice the code of *omerta*, but I do have my own code. One last question. Did you write those letters?''

Tip's white teeth flashed. "With total honesty, I will say no.''

CHAPTER NINE

WHEN ROBERT FORSYTHE LEFT TIP'S ROOM, HE FOUND the cousins still playing backgammon in the conversation pit. From a distance, they looked as much like twins as Hansel and Gretchen did. Their heads were bent over the game and both men wore burgundy jackets, white silk shirts, black slacks. Forsythe decided that when Fredo Clemenza went to the tailor for fittings of his cousin's clothes, he must order two of each garment.

A head lifted, and Funicelli's deep voice called, "Come join us, Robert. We've just finished."

"Believe it or not, I won every game tonight," Clemenza crowed.

The barrister joined them and perched on the arm of a chair. "Is that unusual?"

"Extremely rare," Clemenza told him. "Hard for anyone to win when they play with Anthony."

Clemenza's face was deeply flushed and Forsythe had a hunch that hectic coloring came from more than the thrill of victory. A bourbon bottle sat at the man's elbow and it was more than half-empty. On his cousin's side of the table was a plate with a few crusts, a crumpled napkin, and a tall glass showing traces of milk.

Leaning back against butter-colored leather, Anthony extracted his gold guillotine and clipped a cigar. He smiled at his cousin and then the barrister. "Bet neither of you can guess what I'm planning to do now."

"Take the lift and go up to bed," Clemenza said.

"Not tonight." Funicelli had his cigar going and he heaved his bulk out of the deep chair. As he moved, his foot nudged an object propped against the chair leg. He bent, lifted a handsome black briefcase, and dropped it on the seat of the chair. "Forgot to take that up to my office. Must remember to when I get back."

"Back from where?" Forsythe asked.

"I am about to break habits of a lifetime and take a long and bracing walk."

"You're joking!" his cousin blurted. "You *never* walk."

"While we were playing earlier, I was thinking about Mama Rosa. She could be right. Some exercise may be exactly what I need." Funicelli trotted up the shallow steps and opened a closet door. Pulling a black trench coat out, he put it on. "I was thinking of Lucia, too."

His cousin swung around in his chair. "What has Lucia to do with exercise?"

"You heard the poor little girl when we were dining. She's not allowed any of the things she loves. Mama Rosa won't even let her have a plate of spaghetti. If Lucia is denied all that, I can at least do one thing I loathe."

"When she's delivering, are you also going to have labor pains?" Clemenza asked.

"I've heard some husbands do." Funicelli turned his coat collar up and pulled on black leather gloves.

Clemenza started to pull himself up. "I'll walk with you."

"You get your share of walking, Fredo. Relax and have a nightcap. Oh, nearly forgot. Robert, I'll be wanting to see you when I get back. In my office." He pushed back a sleeve and consulted a watch. "Say an hour and a half."

The barrister consulted his own watch. "That will make it one o'clock."

"Time doesn't make much difference to me. I'm a nighthawk."

Clemenza was pouring another drink. "I think Robert may be hinting he's not and would like to get to bed."

Funicelli chuckled. "Nonsense! Young chap like him."
He opened the front door and waved a gloved hand. "See
you later, Robert."

Much later, Forsythe thought gloomily as he said good
night to Clemenza and mounted the staircase. If time meant
nothing to Funicelli, to hell with the peasants. The lights had
been switched off on the balcony and it was in shadow. He
didn't bother looking for a switch but made his way along it
toward the east wing. The light dimmed even more and he
glanced over the railing. Clemenza was switching off the
lamps in the conversation pit. Was the man actually deserting
his bottle? No, he left a lamp on beside his chair and sank
into the leather, reaching for his glass.

Forsythe was tired and felt irritable. He took a shower,
pulled on striped pajamas, a shabby woolen robe, and his
sandals. Then he sat down at the desk and pulled out the
single drawer. He found a supply of heavy cream-colored
notepaper, matching envelopes, two ball point pens, and a
glassine container of stamps. Using a book as a straight edge,
he divided a sheet into two segments, one narrow, the other
wide. Over the narrow one, he wrote *suspect*, over the wider
motive. He jotted down all the names of the people on the
estate with the exception of Noah Flowers. He took each in
turn and wrote hastily.

Finally, he put down the pen and reached for his pipe. As
he filled it and got it going, he glanced over what he had
written. No lack of suspects, no lack of motives. As Sandy
would say, there was an embarrassment of riches on this
sheet. He found he was wishing Sandy were with him, sitting
near his desk, her gray head cocked to one side, asking what
she called asinine questions. Sandy's questions had helped
to solve a murder several times. He smiled. If Sandy were
here, probably what she would be asking would be, Why
don't you go to bed and to hell with that domineering ass?
Good question, but instead, he'd read his notes over.

Lucia Funicelli. Did Lucia, like Mama Rosa, leave a young
and handsome lover in Sicily? If so, she may possibly want
to gain a widow's share of the Funicelli wealth and lose an

aging husband. Is Lucia capable of this? Tip seems to hint she might be.

Rosa Funicelli. Mothers have murdered sons, but where is the motive? Mama Rosa appears to have her own money and lives exactly as she wishes. Her son certainly doesn't dominate her. It seems to be the reverse.

Fredo Clemenza. Could be tired of living in his cousin's shadow? Tired of playing Funicelli's double and never having much freedom of his own? Possible. With Anthony dead, Fredo could once again indulge in his vices—gambling and chasing young girls. Better ask Anthony how his death would benefit Fredo financially.

Hansel and Gretchen Funicelli. Impossible to think of these two separately. They don't hide their motive. Hatred for their father and revenge for what they consider their mother's murder. One thought: The twins are noted for playing jokes. Could this whole thing be a monstrous hoax?

Felipe Manuel Jesus Delcardo. Best motive thus far. Not only would Tip be free of his hated master but possibility that Mama Rosa, who Tip seems to respect, would fulfill what she regards as her son's wishes. This would be U.S. citizenship and funds for a business for the Delcardo family.

Jacob and Mrs. Flower. Strong motive again: Peony Flower. Doesn't seem likely Jacob would involve his mother in this. But, using her keys, access to Funicelli's office would be possible. Might have typed letters late at night. With the family asleep in soundproofed wings, nothing could be easier. From the little I saw of Jacob Flower, he strikes me as a man who might kill in the heat of anger, but this careful plot to frighten and perhaps kill Funicelli . . .

Shoving back his chair, Forsythe tapped dottle from his pipe bowl into a brass ashtray. He glanced at the digital clock. Twenty after one. Better get along to the office and see whether Funicelli was back. He slid open the drawer and replaced the pen. The sheet of notes, he folded twice and slipped into the pocket of his robe. It wouldn't do to leave that where Tip or Mrs. Flower could stumble upon it. Of course, from what he'd seen of the Mexican, Tip wouldn't have to come on it by chance. No doubt the wily houseman had a thorough look thorough all the family and guest rooms.

Forsythe started to walk toward the hall and then he swung around. His room was much too warm and stuffy for sleeping. He had his hand on the glass door when he stopped. Opening that door would only admit warm humid air from the courtyard. Anthony Funicelli was certainly not much of an architect. He'd situated every sleeping room without outside ventilation. Reluctantly, Forsythe turned the control switch to air conditioning. He hated that flow of artificially cooled air but there was no choice.

When he stepped into the hall, it seemed slightly cooler, and as he swung open the door that led to the balcony, he breathed a sigh of relief. Not only was the air cool but it seemed fresh. It was dark and he paused to allow his eyes to adjust. There was only a dim glow from the single lamp in the conversation pit.

Feeling his way, the barrister headed for the office. As he neared it, he saw that the railing along the lift area was pushed back, the cage was on a level with the balcony, and the bronze filigree door was open. Ah, his host was back and using the forbidden lift.

He called to the dark figure huddled on the bench in the lift, "Walk tire you out, Anthony?"

There was no response, no movement in the cage. Forsythe stepped closer and his sandal brushed something. He bent and stretched out a hand. Then he jerked his hand back. It looked like . . . it was a revolver.

Taking a deep breath, he backed toward the office door. He opened it, fumbled along the wall, then felt a series of switches. Three. He pressed down on all of them. Lights sprang up in the office; lights glinted down on the balcony. They exposed what was in the cage.

Blood had dripped from the bowed head, bright against the white shirt, darker against the burgundy of the jacket. Forsythe gingerly touched a wrist: no pulse. Then he took a closer look at the top of the head. It was a mass of cartilage, bone splinters, oozing gray matter, and congealing blood.

"Funicelli," Forsythe groaned.

While he had been trying to discover who had written to Funicelli, the letter writer had killed. Police, he thought, I must get through to them. His head jerked up. The front door had opened and a figure in a black coat was trotting down into the conversation pit. "Hey, Fredo," a deep voice called, "see you're finally trying the lift. Better not let Mama Rosa catch you."

Forsythe peered from the upturned face of the man below him to the shattered head of the man in the lift. "You'd better come up," he told Anthony Funicelli.

CHAPTER TEN

"MY GOD!" FUNICELLI GULPED AND TURNED HIS back to the lift. "I'd better get a doctor, an ambulance."

"Get on to the police."

"But—"

"Look at the top of his head."

Funicelli looked, swore, and then cried wildly, *"Lucia."*

They both raced into the west wing. Funicelli crashed a door open and reached the bed in two bounds. The figure in that luxurious bed didn't stir. Purple-black hair spread in arabesques over a satin pillow; the duvet and a filmy nightgown had slipped, baring one plump pink-tipped breast. Forsythe waited by the door while the older man touched his wife's chest, the base of her throat. His hairy hand looked incongruous against that milky skin. Lucia made a soft purring sound, a gentle little snore.

"Thank God! She's unharmed." Sinking to his knees, Funicelli sketched a cross over his chest, and seemed about to gather the girl into his arms.

"Don't," Forsythe said sharply. "Let her sleep."

Funicelli nodded and pulled the duvet tenderly up around her chin. He tiptoed to the barrister's side, gestured for him to go into the hall, and turned to fumble for keys to lock the door. Then he sagged limply against the wall.

The barrister took his arm. "Bear up."

"I'm trying. I thought . . . Lucia . . . that beast got the wrong man." Groaning, he buried his face in both hands. "Poor harmless old Fredo."

"The police."

"Yes." Funicelli pushed away from the wall. "I'll phone Sir Cecil. He's only a few miles down the road."

The man was dazed and Forsythe had to lead him back to the office. Funicelli stopped in the doorway and pointed. "The drawer . . . it's been jimmied. That bastard used my gun!"

The shallow drawer across the top of the desk was gaping. Flung on the desktop was the ebony-handled paper knife, its blade bent. Funicelli was reaching for a telephone, but Forsythe grabbed his arm. "Don't touch anything in here. Where's another phone?"

"The conversation pit."

Both men avoided looking at the lift as they stepped out of the office. In the conversation pit, Funicelli slumped into a chair beside the telephone table and picked up the phone. Wandering around, the barrister switched on all the table lamps. When he glanced over his shoulder, he saw Funicelli was gazing into space. "Make that call!"

"I can't seem to remember the number . . . I can't seem to even think. I should remember it. Phone Sir Cecil often enough."

The man was in shock, Forsythe thought, and sweating profusely. Forsythe went to the drinks table and poured a couple of ounces of whiskey into two glasses. He handed one to the other man. "Down this and get that coat off."

Funicelli upended the glass, gulped, coughed, and then sighed heavily. He wiped his sleeve over his damp brow, got up and pulled his trench coat off, and flung it over a chair. "Sorry, Robert. Making a damn fool of myself. Got that number now."

The barrister sank back into the cushioned embrace of fine leather and foam padding. He sipped whiskey and looked at the table where Funicelli and Fredo had played their game earlier. The backgammon case was still open, the dice resting near it. The plate and glass from Funicelli's snack hadn't been moved. There was a sizable amount of bourbon in Clemenza's glass and a few inches in his bottle.

Now, exactly what had happened here?

Clemenza had been downing whiskey and then, for some reason, had used the lift. Why? Anyway, as he rode up in it, the murderer on the shadowy balcony had leaned over the rail, fired one or more shots into the top of his head. . . . No. Not the way that bird cage was constructed. The brass filigree was interwoven fairly tightly. Not a chance of even a crack shot aiming between those metal strands. So, the lift door opened, the railing slid aside, the murderer aimed and fired. . . . *Damn.* Clemenza had been shot in the *top* of the head. To have been shot at that angle, Clemenza had to have been bending forward.

Leaning his head back, Forsythe closed his eyes. Picture the lift. Not only the body on the bench, the entire lift. A picture formed against his eyelids and his eyes snapped open. On the floor, near the polished Gucci loafers . . . a briefcase. A handsome black briefcase. Clemenza had been bending to pick up that—

"Robert! I've spoken to you twice. Did you doze off?"

"Hardly. I was thinking."

Draining his glass, Funicelli bent forward. "Sir Cecil will be here directly. He's phoning the nearest police station, the one in Great Whitsun. I've met the superintendent. Nice chap." He fingered the glass. "I wonder if I should have another shot of this stuff. Does work wonders, but I better not. I'm not used to it. Now Fredo . . ." He broke off and bent his head. "I can't believe it, Robert. We've been together all our lives. And Fredo gave his life for mine."

That's one way of looking at it, Forsythe thought grimly. But I hardly think that even a man as devoted as your cousin would volunteer to have half his head blown off for you.

Pushing back his jacket sleeve, Funicelli checked the time. "Damnation! Where in hell is that man?"

"Take it easy. It hasn't been that long." At that moment, the door chimes sounded musically. "That will be the chief constable now."

"I'll get it." The older man was on his feet. He loped toward the door.

The barrister stayed where he was, watching Funicelli admit an immensely tall man built rather like a stork. His shoulders had a permanent sag, as though from bending politely toward individuals of lesser height. His face also resembled a bird's, a great beak of a nose, very little chin, small bright eyes. As he held out a hand to the barrister, Forsythe noticed those tiny eyes were kind, the baronet's expression mild.

"Ah, Mr. Forsythe," the baronet said. "Great honor to meet you. I've heard much about your, ah, exploits. A pity we must meet under such tragic circumstances." He hovered over Funicelli. "Hadn't you best have a nip of brandy, my dear chap?"

"Just finished some whiskey, Sir Cecil. Where are—"

"Be here soon. Superintendent and his boys. He assured me that Inspector Dolan will be on deck, too. Able men, both of them. Where is the, ah, the body, Anthony?"

"Up there." Funicelli pointed a stubby finger. "In the lift. Do you want to . . ."

The chief constable raised his eyes. "Not much use of me poking around. Not much good at the, ah, the detection end. Mainly an administrator." He added, "Extraordinary, really very strange."

Forsythe wasn't sure whether Sir Cecil was speaking of the site of the murder or of the lift itself. He had a hunch it must be the lift, hanging like a monstrous cage for a huge bird.

Sir Cecil's tiny eyes were now wandering around the conversation pit as though looking for something that was missing. And, for him, something probably was: the location of familiar rooms, of vanished walls. He finally sighed. "Well, might as well be seated." He perched his storklike frame on a sofa and Funicelli sank down at his side. "Anthony, Mr. Lewis will soon have this in hand. Ah, Mr. Forsythe, better warn you to overlook the superintendent's manner. Can be a bit abrupt. Mr. Lewis has been with us for only a short time, but I, ah, understand he's a most astute officer." His voice became even more hesitant. "So grieved to hear about your cousin, Anthony. Mr. Clemenza seemed an, ah, innocuous sort of chap. Last person one would suspect as target for a killer.''

"It was a ghastly mistake, Sir Cecil," Funicelli blurted. "Fredo wasn't the target. I was." He covered his face with a powerful hand.

Looking faintly embarrassed, the baronet awkwardly patted the other man's heavy shoulder. "I know this must be painful, Anthony, but one must bear up. If you are able to help with—" The chimes sounded again and he said, "That must be my colleagues. I'll admit them."

When he opened the front door, a mob of men flooded in. The one in the lead, a fairly tall man, but shorter than the chief constable by a head, stepped to one side to have a word with his superior. Sir Cecil pointed toward the balcony, the other man issued orders, and the mob became an orderly group of uniformed officers, plainclothesmen, and one portly chap grasping a bulging black bag. For a violent death at the Dower House, Forsythe thought, all the stops were being pulled out. Sir Cecil took the man in charge down to the conversation pit and another man followed them.

"Superintendent Lewis and Inspector Dolan," the chief constable said. "I believe both of you have met Mr. Funicelli. And this is a guest, Mr. Robert Forsythe."

Inspector Dolan gave Forsythe a pleasant smile and a brisk handshake. Lewis simply slid glacial eyes over him and turned to Funicelli. Before he had a chance to speak, Funicelli said urgently, "I'll explain later, but I feel my wife is also in danger. Could you get a guard on her door?"

"Barnes," Lewis called. "Mr. Funicelli will show you where his wife's room is. Get your back against her door and stay there until you're relieved."

While Funicelli took the constable up the staircase, Forsythe's eyes wandered along the balcony. Lewis's men were wasting no time. A police photographer was snapping pictures of the lift and its ghastly occupant, another technician was connecting up a small vacuum cleaner, and the doctor was standing by ready for the examination.

"Mr. Forsythe," a voice snapped, and Forsythe turned.

116

Lewis said, "I understand you found the body of the deceased."

"I did."

"You'll be making your statement shortly. But I do want to make one point clear. I know you've received a certain amount of notoriety and you may feel you're more qualified than the police department to handle this case. You are mistaken. I will have no amateur meddling in police business. You'll answer questions and that is all that will be required. Do you understand?"

"You have certainly made your point," the barrister said stiffly.

Forsythe had liked Inspector Dolan at sight. He was as tall as Lewis but had a heavier build. His chin was good; he had intelligent eyes and a pleasant expression. Lewis was a much different type of man. He stood with a stiff military bearing, gray and blond hair bristled above an austere face, and his thin mouth was tight and mulish. All Lewis needed to make him a prototype of a Prussian officer, Forsythe decided, were a monocle and a jagged saber scar.

Lewis shifted his cold eyes to his inspector. "Dolan, you take Mr. Forsythe's statement. After that, he can go to his room. I don't want him underfoot."

Lewis jerked a smart right turn and strode toward the stairs. Sir Cecil made a diffident gesture. "Please don't mind the superintendent's manner. At times, he can be a bit, ah, thorny. But on the whole he's—"

"An astute officer." Forsythe bit off the words.

"That is what I have been led to understand. I have yet to see Mr. Lewis actually, ah, in action." Sir Cecil bent toward the inspector. "Well, Mr. Dolan, I think I may now be excess baggage. Alarm sounded and all is well in hand. To be truthful, I'm getting a bit long in the tooth for being roused from slumber and tumbling straight into a ghastly murder. May be getting a bit old for this position, my boy."

Dolan said stoutly, "Not at all, Sir Cecil."

"Have a request to make, Mr. Dolan. Mr. Funicelli seems at the end of his tether. Perhaps the superintendent should be advised to let him rest for a bit before, ah, grilling him.''

"I'm certain, sir, with Mr. Funicelli and his family, the super will be most tactful.''

"I do hope so. Lucia Funicelli, Anthony's young wife, is in the process of, ah, becoming a mother. And Rosa Funicelli, a dear sensitive lady, is older than I am. You will see . . .''

"Not to worry, sir. They'll be handled gently.''

"Good man. Now, I simply must be getting back to my bed. Charming to meet you, Mr. Forsythe. You must come to dine. I'll ring you. Ah, Mr. Dolan, carry on.''

Forsythe watched the chief constable making his way up the shallow steps to the landing. A constable hastened to hold the door open for him. "Nice chap,'' the barrister said.

"A gentleman of the old school and Sir Cecil happens to be first-rate at his job. He may seem vague but, believe me, I've seen him in action.'' Dolan sank down in a leather chair opposite the barrister and luxuriously wriggled his broad shoulders. "Lovely furniture. Wish I could afford a chair like this.'' He glanced at the balcony and lowered his voice. "Wanted to tell you this, sir. The super didn't speak for all of us at the Great Whitsun station. I will be more than glad to have all the help you can give me.''

"You don't object to amateur meddlers?''

"You're hardly an amateur and you're no meddler. I happen to be friendly with an inspector from the Yard who sings your praises.''

"Beau Brummell?''

"Yes. Every time the wife and I go to London, we drop in to visit Beau and his family. Beau told me how hard it is to get your help and how fast you catch on to items no one else notices. Any tips you got, pass them on.''

Stretching out his leg, Forsythe rubbed at his knee. He reached for the drink tray and poured whiskey into his glass. He raised his brows, but the inspector shook his head. Dolan said briskly, "Now, for your statement. You must be an old hand at this, so I won't prod. Just talk away and I'll have—'' He swung around, spotted the constable, who had opened the door for the chief constable, and called, "Over here, Jarvis. Take notes."

When Jarvis was in place, his pen at the ready, the barrister began. He spoke concisely but omitted nothing from the time he had met Buford Sanderson for a hamburger dinner until Anthony Funicelli had shown him the threatening letters.

At that point, the inspector interrupted. "You say four letters. And all of them written in this house. Does Mr. Funicelli still have them?"

Forsythe hesitated. "The drawer in his office was forced and his revolver removed. I rather think that's where he kept the letters. At the time, I didn't think to check for them."

"Very well. Carry on."

"Mr. Funicelli showed me those letters three days ago. Since then, I've managed to speak with every person on the estate with the exception of Lucia Funicelli." Reaching into the pocket of his robe, Forsythe pulled out the sheet of cream notepaper and handed it to Dolan. "These are notes on my impressions. It's terse and there're many questions and suppositions. If you need me to elaborate, just ask."

Dolan unfolded the sheet and glanced down the page. "Thanks. I'll go over this carefully later. It may help. It looks as though you've come up with any number of motives for the murder of Mr. Funicelli. Strange, getting the wrong man like that. Did this Fredo Clemenza look that much like his cousin?"

"If you couldn't see their faces, it was hard to tell them apart. Fredo had his hair styled like Funicelli's and was wearing clothes identical to his last evening. Even after I turned lights on in the balcony, I still thought the murdered man was Anthony Funicelli."

"Hmm." Dolan pulled at his long underlip. "Tell me about discovering the body."

Patiently, Forsythe related the details. When he had finished, Dolan fastened his eyes on the barrister's face. "Any false notes?"

"One. When I stepped out of the wing my room's in, the air on the balcony was not only cool but seemed fresh . . . as though a door or doors had recently been opened."

The inspector's eyes ranged along the balcony. "Those doors with the red lights over them?"

"Fire exits leading to metal steps."

"I see. Anything else?"

Forsythe rubbed his brow. "That lift. As far as I know the only person in this house who ever uses it is Mr. Funicelli."

Dolan leaned forward. "What about the briefcase?"

"That I can understand. Before Mr. Funicelli left for a walk, he mentioned he was going to take it up to his office. Fredo Clemenza was obviously doing it for him."

"Without being asked?"

"Clemenza didn't have to be asked. He was glad to do any small service he could for his cousin. In fact, that seemed his mission in life. What I can't understand is why the lift? Why didn't he climb the stairs as he usually did?"

The inspector said grimly, "If he had, he might have saved his life. The murderer must have been hiding on that dark balcony, waiting for Mr. Funicelli. If the killer had gotten a good look at Mr. Clemenza's face, he probably would be still alive."

"And Anthony Funicelli might be dead."

Dolan nodded at the constable and the man closed his notebook. "You've been very helpful, sir. You're free to go to your room now. And you probably can use some rest. Good night, sir."

The barrister found he had to grip the handrail to get up the stairs. His leg was aching fiercely and he decided to take a painkiller. He threaded his way among the policemen and one of them turned. "Mr. Forsythe?" The barrister nodded and the man said, "Mr. Funicelli would like to see you, sir. He's in his den." The man pointed at the door next to the office.

Forsythe didn't knock; he opened the door and stepped in. The den was clouded with the rich fumes of fine Havana tobacco. Funicelli, comfortably ensconced in yet another butter-colored leather chair, held a cigar. The superintendent, who was standing, also had a cigar.

Funicelli glanced up. "A moment, Robert. You were saying, Superintendent?"

"I agree with you, sir. I think you're definitely on the right track. May I take those letters with me?"

Funicelli handed over a sheaf of cream-colored envelopes. With the magnate, Forsythe mused, the Prussian officer had changed his manner. He was still as stiff but he acted like a major in the presence of a three-star general. It would appear that the Funicelli wealth and power had a mellowing effect on even Lewis. This was shortly borne out. Funicelli barked, "And the members of my household won't be disturbed?"

"Not until morning, sir." Lewis waved the envelopes. "I'll get my men right onto this lead, sir."

"Do that." Funicelli added, more graciously. "And thank you, Superintendent. I won't forget your courtesy at this trying time."

Forsythe's mouth twisted wryly. Lewis was practically bowing his way out of the room. As the door closed, Funicelli said, "Do be seated, Robert. You look fagged."

The barrister made no movement to take a chair. "I am, and that's why this must be brief. I see the murderer didn't take the letters."

"Overlooked them. Luckily, I'd pushed them under a pile of notepaper. Now, for that brevity you desire. Superintendent Lewis asked me to have a word with you. He cautioned me that you aren't to—"

"Stick my nose into police business."

"I was going to put it more diplomatically, but, yes, that's the idea."

"Do you agree?"

"Yes." Funicelli puffed rapidly at his cigar. "I hate to mention it, but I'm terribly disappointed in you. With your reputation, I expected much more from you. It's only by the

121

grace of a merciful God that bloody fiend didn't kill my Lucia, too."

"Look," Forsythe said tersely, "I came in on this cold only three days ago. I didn't know one person on this estate and I've knocked myself out trying to get to know them, trying to find a motive for the threats."

"Don't try to make excuses. Admittedly, this may be an error in my own judgment. I pride myself on employing people who know their jobs."

"Am I to consider myself discharged?"

"Yes. In fact, the superintendent hopes to have this wrapped up soon. After that, you'll be free to return to London." Funicelli waved his cigar. "Lewis is an extremely discerning officer. Realized immediately, as I did, the culprit. The man you should have been watching instead of badgering my relations."

"Jacob Flower?"

"Of course. Lewis says he knows something about the family. Seems, in this area, they're regarded as strange people, possibly mental cases. All that inbreeding, I suppose. Anyway, now that everything's in competent hands, you might as well get to bed."

Forsythe stood his ground, feeling rage bubbling up within him. He struggled for control. There was more at stake here than wounded pride. "Jacob Flower didn't strike me as a killer. I might see him killing in hot blood but this . . ."

Funicelli lifted heavy dark brows. "How long did you observe him?"

"For only a short time, but—"

"That man positively spouted venom at me. During that conversation about his sister, he raved on and on. Cursed me and made threats." Savagely, Funicelli ground his cigar out. "He shot Fredo to death, and for that, he's going to pay a heavy price!"

Without another word Forsythe swung on his heels and left the room. He stopped abruptly. Two officers were lifting Fredo Clemenza's body onto a body bag. His shattered head was neatly capped in plastic and both his hands were wrapped in plastic film. Forsythe, feeling sick, averted his eyes. Poor, harmless, lonely devil. He found himself wishing the murderer had been right on target.

CHAPTER ELEVEN

It seemed to Robert Forsythe that hardly had his head touched the pillow before he was being shaken awake. He opened heavy eyelids, identified Tip, and closed them again. "Go away."

"I would if I could, but I can't."

"What time is it?"

"Ten forty-five. And that's A.M., in case you're confused. Sorry to disturb you, but the master has summoned all members of the household for a conference. And the gendarmes are here in the person of a heel-clicking superintendent named Lewis."

The barrister forced his eyes open and threw back the duvet. "Have you been interviewed?"

"An Inspector Dolan had a few words with me earlier. Nothing much I could tell him. After you left my room last night, I didn't stir out of the lower west." The houseman adjusted his mess jacket and sleeked back already sleek hair. "Kind of a decent sort, that Dolan. I can't say the same about the guy here now."

"Most discerning, Tip. As you may find, Superintendent Lewis also has two rules. One for Funicelli and no doubt his family, and quite another for anyone else." Forsythe dangled long legs from the edge of the bed and reached for his robe.

"So, you didn't hear about Fredo Clemenza until this morning."

"I couldn't believe my ears when the inspector told me." Tip shook a baffled head. "Case of mistaken identity."

Forsythe looked up at the younger man. "Did you ever see Clemenza using that lift?"

"Never. Poor chap thought it was a joke and raced up and down the staircase. Wonder what he was doing in it?"

"That seems to be the vital question."

The houseman nodded, opened the door, and then called back. "If you're hungry, let me know once the conference is over. No one wanted breakfast, but I can whip some up for us."

Forsythe didn't hurry. He took a leisurely shower, shaved, pulled on tweeds and heavy brogues, and slung his Burberry over an arm. From the balcony, he spotted the conference site. The lift was now resting once again on the platform but had been shrouded with a black tarp. In the conversation pit, all the Funicellis were gathered. The twins, wearing jeans and red ponchos, were huddled on a sofa, and on the one opposite, Funicelli sat, his wife on his left, his mother on his right. Tip stood near the fireplace, and Lewis, looking much at ease, relaxed in a chair. He was puffing on a cigar, and as Forsythe neared the group, the rich aroma of Havana floated toward him.

No one greeted the barrister, but Gretchen slid to one side, patting the seat beside her. Forsythe sat down between the twins and looked from one heart-shaped face to the other. Their fine features were as stony as Mrs. Flower's. He glanced at the opposite sofa. Funicelli's eyes were darkly circled but he was nattily dressed in a brown suit, a tan shirt, and a brown figured tie. Flung across the back of the sofa was a vicuña overcoat, with beige leather gloves resting on top of it. Both the women were in housecoats. Mama Rosa's was black and severely tailored, but Lucia had selected a romantic daffodil-yellow creation with floods of ivory lace. Around the girl's shoulders, purple-black hair fell loosely and she looked fresh, well rested, and gorgeous. Forsythe noticed that Lewis had his eyes glued to her lovely face.

Funicelli moved restlessly. "We're all here now, Superintendent. Could you get on with it?"

Lewis tore his eyes away from Lucia, cleared his throat, and spoke. It sounded like a prepared speech. "I should like to offer my condolences to the members of Mr. Clemenza's family. Although it is hard to find comfort at a moment like this, I do have some to give you. My officers and I have charged Jacob Flower with the murder of Mr. Fredo Clemenza. As a result of this fast arrest, I have no need to disturb you further. I realize you are shocked and saddened and any who wish to leave this house may do so. We would like your addresses and a telephone number where you can be reached." He glanced around. "That is all."

"Not quite," Gretchen said sharply. She jerked forward. "You can't arrest a man simply because he dislikes my father."

"Leave police business to the police," her father said just as sharply.

"Anthony." His mother put a restraining hand on Funicelli's brown sleeve. "I happen to agree with Gretchen." She asked the superintendent, "Do you have evidence against Jacob Flower?"

"Of course." Lewis butted his cigar and came to his feet. "Mrs. Funicelli, I assure you if we didn't have evidence, Mr. Flower wouldn't be in jail in Great Whitsun now."

"What evidence?" Mama Rosa asked imperiously.

"Not only did Mr. Flower make threats against your son but the man is obviously a maniac. While I was questioning him last night, he attacked me and had to be handcuffed."

Forsythe said quietly, "I hardly think that constitutes sufficient evidence for charging a suspect."

Lewis gave the barrister a look of complete dislike. "I forgot we have an expert on law among us. No, Mr. Forsythe, that did not constitute sufficient evidence, but in the greenhouse at the rear of this house, we found evidence that does." He turned his back on Forsythe. "At this point, sir, I'm afraid that is all I can say."

"And that is quite enough." Resting a genial hand on the policeman's shoulder, Funicelli steered him toward the front door. "I compliment you and your officers on rapid and efficient work. Nothing can return my cousin to us, but we do have the satisfaction of knowing his killer will be punished. And we are also reassured about our own safety. I appreciate this, Superintendent Lewis."

"A matched pair," Hansel hissed into the barrister's ear.

Forsythe nodded and glanced at the two women opposite him. Mama Rosa had lighted a cigarette and was smoking it in quick jerky puffs. If she was upset, however, that was the only sign of agitation. Her heart-shaped face was serene. "Hansel and Gretchen," she said, "your father and I are going in to Great Whitsun shortly to make funeral arrangements. Do you feel . . . would you like Fredo's body to be sent back to Chicago for burial?"

Gretchen said hoarsely, "It makes no difference. I don't think Fredo would care where you bury him."

Her grandmother bent toward her. "You can cry, you know. Sometimes it does help."

"How?" Gretchen lunged to her feet. "You don't give a damn about Fredo. All you and father will do is tidy up the details, give Fredo a nice funeral. You know what I hate? Except for Hansel and me, not one damn soul in this family cares that Fredo is dead!"

"Gretchen," Mama Rosa cried.

However, Gretchen was gone, taking the stairs in great bounds, with Hansel at her heels. Mama Rosa shook her head and touched her daughter-in-law's arm. "Now, don't get upset, dear. Gretchen didn't mean what she said."

Lucia didn't look upset. One chubby hand was patting the tiers of lace on her skirt. "Perhaps Gretchen is right," the girl murmured. "Oh, I feel sad, but I really didn't know Fredo that well. Will you miss your nephew?"

Forsythe was interested in hearing how the older woman would field that question, but she was spared by her son's return. Funicelli hugged his wife and kissed her cheek. "Are you all right, angel?"

Lucia moved away from his arms. "I want to go to Great Whitsun with you and Mama Rosa."

"Not today, darling." He added coaxingly, "If you're a

127

good girl, we'll drive up to London tomorrow. Just you and me. We'll have a nice dinner and go to the theater.''

She shook her head and pouted rebelliously. Her husband sent a helpless look at his mother and she said briskly, "You go back to bed and rest, Lucia, and as a special treat, Tip will take you a tray with anything you wish."

Lucia's eyes glowed. "Spaghetti? With meat sauce?"

Her mother-in-law sighed. "I suppose one serving will do no harm."

"And I want dessert. Chocolate cake and—"

"Anything you wish. Tip . . ."

"Si, Señora Rosa." The Mexican had stood so motionlessly that Forsythe had forgotten he was there. Now, he moved and walked toward the west wing. "I will make up a tasty meal for Señora Lucia."

Funicelli was consulting his watch. "We'd better get going, Mother."

"I'll get dressed. Anthony, Mr. Forsythe did try very hard to prevent this from happening. It certainly isn't his fault that dreadful Flower man killed your cousin. He must be rewarded for his services."

"He will be." Funicelli waited until his mother was heading toward the east wing. Then, for the first time that morning, he looked directly at the barrister. "Robert, you must forgive my remarks last night. At that time, I was terribly distraught. Lewis said he would like you to remain in the house today. But tomorrow . . ." His voice trailed off. "Send me your bill and I'll have a check in the mail. And thank you."

The barrister rose and slipped on his Burberry. "No thanks are in order and there will be no fee."

Funicelli reddened and then shrugged and turned away. Cold, Forsythe thought, as icy as the blast of wind that whistled around him as he stepped out onto the driveway. It was not raining, but the sky was leaden with the threat of a downpour. Turning up his collar, Robert jammed both hands into his pockets. At the corner of the manor, he hesitated, and then walked back along the stucco addition. He had forgotten to remove from the van the Churchill replicas he had bought.

As he passed the knot garden, he glanced at an area near the garage where a figure in a red tartan jacket was furiously spading at packed soil. Forsythe located the boxes and pushed them into his pockets. Again he hesitated. After a moment, he walked toward Noah Flower. He noticed a fair-sized greenhouse behind the turned earth. As he drew closer, he spotted the tiny black dog sprawled on the grass, happily gnawing at Noah's leather cap.

The man glanced up. Straw-colored hair blew around a face that, despite the chill, was flushed and running with sweat. Forsythe wished him a good morning but Noah didn't respond. He did stop working and leaned against the spade, however. "Mister," he finally blurted, "what's happened and where did those men take Jacob?"

Forsythe was wishing he had headed away from this child-man. He said gently, "Didn't your mother explain?"

The untidy head shook. "Mommie was crying. After those men took Jacob away, she cried. Only other time Mommie cried is when Peony . . . She told me to go ahead and work. Spade the kitchen garden over, she said. The Lord doesn't love slackers, Mommie said. Will they bring Jacob back?"

The barrister had no answer. Divert him, he thought; children are easily diverted. "Tell me about your dog. Does Blackie know any other tricks?"

"Sure he does! Lots. Blackie, play dead!"

The dog stopped gnawing the cap, flopped down on his side, closed his eyes. "Isn't he smart?" his owner asked proudly.

"Indeed he is. He's a fine little fellow."

"And good, mister, a real good dog. But he pees a lot. Sometimes I got to get up and take him out a couple of times a night. If I don't Blackie piddles on the rug and Mommie doesn't like that." Noah's wide face twisted with anxiety. "Mister, do you think he's sick?"

Damn, Forsythe thought, he's lost both his sister and his brother. Now he's afraid he may lose his dog. Picking the animal up, the barrister felt the moist black nose, pulled back the skin and looked at the eyes. Under the thick hair, the dog's bones felt like those of a bird, tiny and fragile. "I'm not a vet, Noah, but I'd say this chap is in fine shape. Some dogs have trouble controlling their bladders, you know. Maybe you shouldn't give him water before you go to bed."

"He drinks a lot of water, mister. But I'll do what you say. You're a nice man. Not like that . . ." Noah waved an expressive hand at the heavy wooden door in the rear wall of the courtyard.

Forsythe handed the dog to his master and Noah cradled him in his arms. "Is your mother at home now?"

"Mommie said she was going to tidy up the cottage. That man told Mommie never to set foot in his house again. Said we have to move. Maybe he doesn't want me spading his garden." Noah darted a fearful look at the wooden door, as though it might be thrown open and Anthony Funicelli would come charging out at him.

"You do what your mother told you, Noah. I'll go down and talk with her and see what can be done."

Noah's eyes lit up and he beamed down at the barrister. "Maybe you can make those men bring Jacob home again."

Having no reassuring answer, Forsythe turned away. Noah shouted at him, "Mister, those people do funny things, don't they?"

Not funny, amusing, Forsythe thought as he stepped onto the gravel of the driveway. The heavily carved door of the manor was opening and Mama Rosa, bundled in lustrous mink, stepped out. She was followed by her son. He turned the collar of the vicuña coat up around his ears and tugged on matching gloves. "You wait here, Mother. I'll bring the car around."

Funicelli brushed past the barrister as though the younger man was invisible. His mother raised a hand and gave a regal wave. Forsythe waved back and continued down the driveway under the canopy of bare oak branches creaking dismally in the wind. It was a long walk and seemed even longer because he walked slowly, favoring his bad leg. He had reached the gate house when Funicelli's sleek Mercedes rolled past, slowed, and turned off toward Safrone.

* * *

As the barrister walked up the path, the door of the cottage opened wide, as though Mrs. Flower had sensed his arrival. Her face was bright and eager, but as she realized who her caller was, the eagerness dimmed and vanished. "Mr. Forsythe. I thought they might be bringing Jacob. . . . There's been a terrible mistake made. The police took Jacob. . . ." Catching up a corner of her apron, she twisted it in both hands. "Come in, sir. The wind's so cold."

"It is. I was just speaking with Noah, Mrs. Flower. Do you think he should be working in that wind?"

"He's a healthy boy. And it's better for him to work than to stay in here all day. Noah doesn't understand, you see; he doesn't know why his brother was taken away. I've been trying to keep my mind off it by cleaning up the house."

Mrs. Flower had indeed been working. All the clutter had been cleared away and the boots were lined up against a wall like soldiers. The place looked like a medieval dungeon. Mrs. Flower took his coat. "I'm making a pot of tea. Would you care for a cuppa?"

Forsythe nodded and followed the woman past the forlorn huddle of chairs, past the oval frame where the late Mr. Flower glowered, to the kitchen. The table had been scrubbed until the pine gleamed. The only sign of cheer was a kettle puffing steam on the stove. As Mrs. Flower poured water and measured tea leaves, she talked rapidly, as though looking for release.

"The police came late last night, Mr. Forsythe. Hammering on the door and getting us out of bed. The man in charge is a spawn of Satan—"

"Superintendent Lewis?"

"That was his name. He shouted at Jacob and called him awful things. And Jacob, his devil got loose and he flew at the man and would have knocked him flying if the other policemen hadn't grabbed him. They put handcuffs on my boy and they took him away." Her hand was shaking and she nearly dropped a jug of milk.

Forsythe jumped up and took the pitcher from her hand. "Sit down, Mrs. Flower, I'll pour."

He poured brown steaming tea into pottery mugs and set

131

one down in front of the woman. Cradling the warmth of the other mug in both hands, he leaned against the sink. "I understand that the police found some evidence against your son. Do you know what it is? Lewis said they uncovered it in the greenhouse."

She had been blowing on her tea. She set down the mug and said grimly, "I should know. That spawn of Satan waved it in my face, in my son's face. Pieces of paper in a plastic bag, it was. The police said they were letterheads."

Ah, Forsythe thought, four letterheads from four threatening letters. Aloud, he asked, "Where in the greenhouse did they find them?"

"In my son's jacket, they said. An old one he keeps in the greenhouse. It's a tartan wool jacket, like the one his brother wears, only green. Lady Safrone gave the boys those, the year before she died. Noah's is still good, but Jacob is awful hard on his clothes and his jacket is nearly worn out. The police said there was a hole in a pocket and those pieces of paper had slid down between the lining and the woolen material. Jacob swore he knew nothing about them, that someone must have stuck them there, but the police wouldn't listen."

Forsythe stroked his chin. It looked as though the police had ample reason for an arrest. Jacob Flower had quarreled with Anthony Funicelli, had made threats in front of witnesses; the letters were written much as Jacob talked, and the letterheads were found in his jacket. . . . He jerked himself back to the kitchen in the Flower cottage. Mrs. Flower was still talking. "—and then they asked me questions. If Jacob had left this house last night. I told them 'no,' that all of us work hard and that we all go to bed early and sleep heavily. Of course, Noah has to get up to walk that dog of his. Nuisance that animal is, but Noah sets great store by him and—"

"Did you hear your younger son leave the house last night?"

"No. But then I never hear Noah get up." She sighed. "I

had to tell the police that. I wanted to protect Jacob, but I can't lie.''

Forsythe drained his cup and poured fresh tea. "Does Jacob know anything about firearms?''

"He's never held a gun in his hands in his entire life. Our faith doesn't hold with that. Guns are to kill." She looked up at him. "Tip told me you're a barrister, sir. I was wondering. Do you think you could . . .''

"If I were free to, I certainly would, Mrs. Flower. But very likely I'll be called as a witness and I can't represent your son's interest.''

There was silence and then she said slowly. "I see that. I shouldn't have asked but I don't know where to turn. Mr. Funicelli has ordered us out of this house." She looked around the bleak room with an expression of anguish. "This has always been the Flower home. I was born here and my mother and father died here. I don't know where to go, how to earn a living. And there's Noah. Who will employ him? Who will look after him when I'm gone?''

The barrister put a comforting hand on her shoulder. "I'm certain Sir Cecil will see you come to no harm.''

The muscles under his hands tensed. "Flowers don't take charity. Never have and never will.''

"There is something I *can* do to help. I can arrange for a solicitor and a barrister to defend your son.''

Hope flashed across her face. "Can you get good ones?''

"The best. Eugene Emory is my friend and a very skillful barrister.''

"Then he'll be expensive," she said shrewdly.

Extremely expensive, Forsythe thought. But he would provide the funds for Gene's defense. Perhaps Mrs. Flower was following his thoughts. She said stiffly, "I haven't much money set aside but I'll pay the bills if it takes the rest of my life." Then she repeated, "Flowers do *not* take charity.''

Her brief moment of defiance was gone. She slumped in her chair, gazing unseeingly across the room. "It's all in

God's hands now. I'll pray for guidance and He will lead the way."

Forsythe picked up his Burberry and felt in a pocket. Pulling out a box, he took it back to the table and set it down beside Mrs. Flower's mug. "For you," he said gently. "Use it for vinegar."

With trembling hands, she extracted the replica of Churchill and turned the key. Music tinkled out, providing, for a few moments, a note of cheer in that barren room. When Forsythe left the gate house, she was clutching the gaudy object to her bosom like a talisman.

"I'll pray for you," she told him softly.

And I'll need those prayers, Forsythe said grimly and silently as he retraced his steps.

The gutted manor wasn't much more cheerful than the Flowers' cottage had been. As the barrister made his way up to the east wing, there was no one in sight. He stopped in his room to hang his Burberry and tuck the other music box into his pigskin case. Then he walked down to the twins' studio. Gretchen opened the door. She was attired in a white bikini, but this time, a minute band of material was drawn over her small breasts.

"If it isn't our sleuth! And, judging from Father's attitude, a most disappointing one. Hansel, come say hello."

Hansel, wearing bikini trunks, appeared from around the corner of the partition. He greeted the barrister effusively. Both the twins had high color and seemed possessed by a frenetic gaiety.

"We're going to have a final dip," Hansel called. He tapped a wicker basket sitting among wood chips on his sister's worktable. "And we have a picnic lunch. Care to join us?"

"That's an offer I can't refuse," the barrister told them. He took a deep breath. The air was warm and smelled pleasantly of cedar and lemon and turpentine.

In the courtyard, it was difficult to picture the cold and cutting wind above the glass roof. The Garden of Eden, Forsythe thought, all it lacked was an apple tree. He pictured a

134

lusciously naked Lucia Funicelli offering her husband a red and rosy apple. There his imagination failed. He couldn't picture Funicelli, with his hard worldly face, in the role of a naïve Adam.

Hansel nudged his arm. "Swim first. Funeral meats later. You'll find trunks—"

"In the cabana," Forsythe said, and picked his way between palms to the pink and white structure near the rear of the courtyard. He shed his tweeds and brogues, donned trunks, and headed for the lagoon. The twins hadn't waited. They were playing water polo with a beach ball, and their brown bodies dipped and surged like sleek young seals. With no hesitation, he dove into the pool and stroked strongly down the length of it. Deserting their game, Hansel and Gretchen gamboled along beside him. He expected them to dive and pull him under, but they didn't. He swam several laps and then circled around to the edge. Pulling himself up, he perched on the tile lip of the pool. Gretchen swam over and treaded water near him. She eyed the white scars on his knee. "Does swimming bother your leg?"

"The reverse. Makes it feel better." Reaching for a towel, Forsythe rubbed at his hair. "The *final* swim?"

"We're getting the hell out of here tomorrow." She braced a hand on the side of the pool and floated. "Have you found out what the superintendent's damning evidence was yet?"

"What makes you think I was looking for it?"

"Come off it, sleuth. You didn't fall for that crock about Jacob Flower any more than we did." Pulling herself up beside him, she started to towel her dripping hair. "I'll admit I know little about the man, but I have talked, or tried to talk, to his mother. Those people simply drip religion. Can you see someone like Jacob writing dirty letters to Father and then lurking around with a revolver in his hand?"

"You win." Forsythe grinned down at her. "I'll tell all."

135

"Get over here, Hansel! Mr. Forsythe is going to come clean on that evidence."

When Hansel was sitting on the other side, the barrister told them what the police had found in the greenhouse. Hansel snorted. "Jacob has got to be *stupid*. Why didn't he flush those letterheads down the toilet or burn them?"

Gretchen bent forward and glared at her brother. "Because, you ass, he didn't write those letters. Someone's built a neat frame. Which means that someone is still gunning for our dear old dad."

"Hallelujah!" Hansel chortled. "Oh, day of rejoicing. May his arm be strong and his aim be true."

Forsythe was now toweling his shoulders. "His sights may be on your stepmother, too."

Both twins sobered and Hansel muttered, "I'd forgotten about Lucia. But she's safe right now. Shortly after you left this morning, a brawny policewoman arrived to stay right at Lucia's side. Even with Jacob tucked away in a cell, Father's taking no chances. He told Mama Rosa that as soon as this is straightened out, he's taking Lucia to Chicago."

Gretchen's lips were quivering. "And Fredo will be buried in an English cemetery and no one will ever have to worry about his drinking and gambling again."

"Or his wenching," Hansel said soberly. "Grandmother is glad to be rid of him, and he was only an albatross to Father. The poor old bugger didn't have a friend in the world."

"Except us." She bent her head and sodden hair fell over her face.

Putting an arm around her shoulders, Forsythe said, "Your grandmother might have been right about one thing. It could help to cry."

"If I started crying, I doubt I'd be able to stop." She sprang to her feet. "Let's chow down."

The contents of the basket were spread on the table and Forsythe was regaled with iced lemon tea, Greek salad, and freshly baked bread. "I could learn to like this diet," he said as he reached for another slice of bread. Spearing a morsel

136

of feta, he asked cautiously, "You know about Fredo's history with young girls?"

Hansel shrugged. "It was a badly kept secret."

"Why on earth was this man, with this vice, put in charge of children?"

Gretchen spooned out more salad. "Because Mama Rosa knew that Fredo would never touch a hair on our heads, let alone molest us. He was a Sicilian, you know."

"Another code of honor?"

"A rigid one. Hansel and I were family. The only time Fredo ever touched me was when he held my hand to comfort me while they operated on Hansel." Her hand, grasping a fork, trembled, and she forced a note of hectic gaiety into her voice. "Robert, I'd like a promise. But, one moment, I've something for you that I made yesterday." Fishing in the basket, she pulled out a small carving and handed it to him. "A going-away present."

The barrister looked wonderingly down at it. This was even cleverer than the carving she had made for Tip. On a tiny base was a figure attired in a flowing robe and with a mass of high piled curls. Minute hands clasped an old-fashioned scale and the weight seemed to be dragging the arms down. Under a wig, a few skillful strokes of a knife had fashioned a long face remarkably like his own. He turned it over and said, "You've carved your name and date on the base. Thank you, Gretchen. When you're famous, I'll have this to prove I once knew you." He raised his head. "What promise do you want?"

She took a deep breath. "Protect Lucia and find the bastard who killed Fredo but—"

"Don't stop him from shooting Father," Hansel finished.

Forsythe got to his feet and looked down at the two young faces. "I promise I'm going to do my best to find Fredo's killer, but I must do my best not only to protect Lucia but also your father."

"A qualified answer," Hansel groaned. "Well, what else can you expect from a lawyer?"

137

Later, as Forsythe made his way back to his room, he cradled the robed and wigged figure in one hand. Indeed, at times, the scales of justice did prove weighty.

CHAPTER TWELVE

For the remainder of that day, Forsythe stayed in his room. Through the daylight hours, the eternal summer streaming in through glass doors didn't vary and the only way of measuring the passing time was by the digital clock.

The barrister decided the best thing to do to pass some of that time was to get some much-needed rest. He stripped off his clothes, pulled on his old woolen robe, and stretched out on the bed. He dozed for a while but his sleep was uneasy, and finally he gave it up and took the chair by the desk. He located his telephone charge card, consulted his address book, and dialed Eugene Emory's chambers in London.

The sound of his friend's familiar voice came as somewhat of a relief. Tersely, he filled in the details of Jacob Flower's arrest.

"You'd like me to undertake his defense?" Emory asked.

"I would."

"You do believe the man's innocent?"

"Yes."

"Does Flower have a solicitor on deck?"

"No. I was hoping that perhaps you—"

Emory chuckled. "Rather putting the cart before the horse, isn't it?"

"There's only the man's mother to take control, and Mrs.

Flower is completely unworldly. She wouldn't even know where to start.''

"Well, in that case, we'll do something highly unusual. The noted barrister will arrange for a solicitor." Emory asked, "This means a great deal to you, doesn't it?"

"It does, Gene."

"Rest easy. I'll put the wheels in motion."

"About your fee . . ."

"Robert, you can forget a fee. I owe you a couple."

"And the solicitor?"

There was a pause and then Emory laughed again. "The best. I'll speak with Willy Seton. He owes you one, too, doesn't he?"

Thinking of Willis Seton and the Dancer case, Forsythe grinned. "He does indeed. No need to remind Willy. He'll remember Amyas Dancer and the body in Mandalay."

A few moments later, the phone rang. Forsythe reached for it, hoping he would hear Sandy's voice. However, it was Sir Cecil Safrone, speaking slowly and hesitantly. "Mr. Forsythe," the chief constable said. "No doubt you are wondering why I am calling you. Have I interrupted your dinner?"

The barrister assured Sir Cecil he hadn't, and then wondered whether he was about to receive an invitation to dine with the baronet. After interminable ah-ing, however, it seemed dinner was the last thing on the older man's mind. Forsythe decided he might just as well try to get a little information from the chief constable. "Sir Cecil," he said, "do you know any of the details of the investigation that you can pass on?"

The baronet answered readily. "Evidence was uncovered when a search was made of the outbuildings. In the greenhouse, an officer found letterheads—"

"I've heard about those letterheads from Mrs. Flower."

"Ah, then you'll be interested in time of death and fingerprints and so on."

"Precisely."

"The revolver, the paper knife, and the surfaces on the

140

desk were wiped clean. Dr. Soames has estimated time of death at midnight or shortly after."

"I see," Forsythe said, and he did. It looked as though the only solid evidence against Jacob Flower were the letterheads found in his jacket.

Sir Cecil was speaking again. "Perhaps, Mr. Forsythe, I am being highly unorthodox in speaking with you, but I am a trifle . . . ah, perturbed."

"How may I help?" Forsythe prodded.

"I feel you are a man of much sensitivity and, of course, you have a distinguished reputation for solving crimes. I've just returned from seeing young Jacob at Great Whitsun and I was wondering. . . . Do you feel Mr. Lewis has been a bit, ah, precipitous?"

It was Forsythe's opinion that Lewis was a perfect ass, but he said, "I don't feel Flower is the murderer. In fact, I've just made arrangements for a friend to undertake the man's defense."

"Then we are in agreement. Admittedly, the evidence Mr. Lewis uncovered makes it look black for the lad, but I've known Jacob since he was a toddler. Mrs. Flower, during the last difficult years of my mother's life, was extremely kind to her. It's possible this emotional involvement with the Flower family is clouding my judgment." There was a long pause and then the baronet said in a voice in which there was no hesitancy, "But I am going to trust my instincts, which you seem to share."

Forsythe cleared his throat. "You must realize that my own knowledge of Jacob Flower is limited. There is a possibility that we're mistaken. Could you tell me what you base your feeling on?"

"Jacob is a very bright chap, Mr. Forsythe. His mother insisted he leave school when he was barely sixteen and I begged her to allow me to fund more education for the lad. But the Flowers are proud and independent and Jacob was eager to find work, assume his father's role, and raise his brother and baby sister."

The chief constable was taking a long time to get to the point. Forsythe prodded him again. "I gather you think Jacob's too intelligent to hold on to those letterheads and to hide them in his own jacket?''

"Exactly. And there is also the lad's character to consider. Jacob has a bad temper, always has had, but I can't see him killing or using a gun to do that killing. I have told Mr. Lewis some of my thoughts, but he is adamant and I don't feel I can actively interfere. But the thought occurred that if you and I are right, the killer is still in that house and that Anthony and Lucia are still in danger.''

"Provision has been made for Lucia Funicelli's safety," Forsythe pointed out.

"Yes. Mr. Lewis says he's detailed WPC Evans to stay with Lucia. But there is still Anthony to consider. Would you . . . do you think you could keep an eye out, do what you can to protect Anthony?''

Forsythe's mouth set in a hard line. "I'm afraid that is out of my hands, Sir Cecil. Mr. Funicelli has made it quite clear he expects me to leave the Dower House tomorrow.''

"A stubborn man, Mr. Forsythe." Sir Cecil sighed heavily. "And I fear that Mr. Lewis is quite overawed by Anthony's wealth and position and isn't thinking clearly. Well, tomorrow I shall take a more active role in this investigation. Most definitely, I will have a word with both Anthony and the superintendent. I would like to thank you for arranging counsel, although I am at a loss to understand your motivation.''

"Simple justice," Forsythe said. "I'll also admit that I like and pity Mrs. Flower and Noah.''

"Don't worry about Mrs. Flower and young Noah. I'll take their welfare in hand. I've a gardener's cottage standing empty and—''

"Mrs. Flower won't accept charity, sir.''

Sir Cecil laughed. "I'm well aware how stiff-necked she is, but I won't be offering charity. I'll be offering employment. I am also willing to defray any expenses connected with Jacob's defense if that should be necessary.''

"That's well in hand, Sir Cecil.''

"You're a decent chap, Mr. Forsythe.''

As Forsythe replaced the receiver, he decided Sir Cecil

Safrone was not only a decent chap but that Inspector Dolan's assessment of him was correct. Kind and gentlemanly he was, and when necessary, the chief constable could be decisive.

Forsythe sighed, massaged his aching knee, and reached for a sheet of notepaper. The room seemed dim and he glanced toward the glass doors. During his conversation with the baronet, the overhead lights in the courtyard had switched off. Turning on the desk lamp, he proceeded to fill the sheet with the notes he had made earlier on suspects and motives. This time he omitted Jacob and his mother. He tried to put it down exactly as he had on the paper now in Inspector Dolan's keeping.

When this was finished, he took a fresh sheet and drew a plan of the house and additions, inking in all the exits. So many exits: the front door opening into the manor, four doors opening on to the courtyard, one from the rear of the manor, two from the far ends of the wings, the rear one opposite the kitchen garden, the two fire exits opening directly onto the balcony. Looking down at the sketch, he shook his head. A person with keys could enter this house by any number of doors. Hopeless!

For the remainder of the evening, the only human contact Forsythe had was with Tip. The houseman appeared carrying a tray, set it down on the corner of the desk, took a look at the papers spread on that desk, and said, "When you didn't ring, I thought I'd better bring some sustenance. Burning the midnight oil?"

Glancing up at the man's heavy features, the sleek hair resembling a bandleader in the thirties, Forsythe grinned. "Hardly midnight. Barely after eight. The family had their dinner yet?"

"Not a formal meal." Tip shrugged a white-clad shoulder. "Been running all over the place with trays. The master and the lady cop are with fair Lucia, guarding her from things that go bong in the night. Mama Rosa is having a solitary repast in her sitting room. Thank God for the twins. They're probably stirring up a pureed mess in their studio. I also had to make up a guest room near Mama Rosa's quarters for the master. The lady cop is going to bunk on a cot in Lucia's bedroom.''

Forsythe arched his brows. "Surely there's an extra bedroom in the upper west wing for Anthony."

"The extra bedroom's been converted into a palatial nursery and the master doesn't fancy sleeping in a bassinet or crib." Tip poured steaming coffee from an insulated jug. "Have you seen the lady cop?"

"Not as yet."

"Not a bad-looking wench. Great legs, but she's at least six foot and no doubt could throw me over her shoulder. Oh, nearly forgot. The master asked me to inquire what time you require a lift to the station tomorrow. Seems to be panting to see you leave."

"I'm no further use to him, Tip. He has Lewis in his pocket."

The houseman laughed. "I've got a hunch the superintendent is hoping Mr. Funicelli will take him on as head of his security force, with an enormous salary in American bucks."

"I shouldn't be surprised, but you're a disgusting cynic." Forsythe asked, "What time is the first train to London due?"

"Eight forty-five in the morning. There's not another until four in the afternoon."

"Better make it the early one, Tip."

"Right. Eat hearty." As the Mexican left, a few words drifted back. "Wish I were leaving with you."

While Forsythe consumed prime rib and a baked potato, he looked his notes over. Nothing fresh here. He was tempted to ring up his secretary and talk for a time, but there was nothing Sandy could do to help. He was much on his own. About ten, he gave up, stuck the tray in the hall, locked the door, and showered. Then he slid into bed. His leg was so painful that he had to go to the bathroom for a painkiller. The pain dulled and he slipped into deep slumber. His last conscious thought was that he simply must visit his physician and agree to the operation on his knee.

He twisted and turned, dreaming of a heavyset man bending over him, a scalpel in one hand, a wide white grin on his face. Above the white coat was Tip's broad face and the scalpel turned into a paring knife. Forsythe fought to avoid that blade and woke to find sheets twisting around his sweaty body, the duvet tumbled to the floor.

Too hot, he thought drowsily, and stumbled across the room. He slid the glass door back and warm fragrant air puffed into his face. Damn, he'd forgotten to switch on the air conditioning. Stepping out onto the balcony, he held his pajama top away from his damp chest. Leaning against the railing, he gazed blearily down at the courtyard. Lamp standards cast pools of light, fairy lights gleamed in the water of the lagoon, and . . . Forsythe bent forward, rubbing his eyes.

I'm still dreaming, he thought. Only this time, I'm in Mama Rosa's sitting room looking at votive lights casting flickers upward across a painting done by a dead man. However, he felt the metal of the railing clenched in one hand, his nails biting painfully into the palm of his other hand.

Around the base of the palm tree directly below were two hands: large hands clenched in agony, nails biting into the bark of that tree.

Gethsemane.

CHAPTER THIRTEEN

Afterward, Forsythe retained no memory of leaving his room, racing down the hall to the spiral staircase, unlocking the outer door, entering the courtyard. His memory didn't spare him from what was waiting in that courtyard, however. Near the far end of the lagoon was the body of a tiny black dog. The body of the dog's master was sprawled, facedown, hands laced around the trunk of the tall palm.

Forsythe bent over Noah Flower, feeling frantically for signs of life. When he straightened, his hands were covered with blood but his mind was working clearly. He backed away, looking at his watch. Three minutes after midnight. The boy hadn't been dead for long. The body was warm and the blood hadn't started to congeal. The back of the red tartan jacket was ripped and sodden with warm blood. Knifed, the barrister thought, knifed a number of times.

Wiping both hands down his pajama top, he circled around to the end of the lagoon. Splotches of blood had sunk darkly into white sand; a butcher knife was near the dog's body. He examined the dog. Blackie hadn't been knifed. His neck was bent at an angle, as though the tiny creature's neck had been broken. However, the blood had to have come from Noah Flower. So . . . the dog kicked to death, the boy sinking to his knees beside the animal, the knife rising over Noah's broad back. Forsythe took a deep breath. Noah had been only a child with a child's reactions. He'd felt sharp pain in his back; he was bewildered. He hadn't tried to fight back. Noah had crawled away, leaving a trail of blood behind him. Near that palm, the murderer had caught him and finished his bloody work.

Forsythe was biting down so hard on his lower lip that he felt blood oozing. An intensity of blind red rage that he never before had felt was sweeping through him. Easy, he warned himself, this won't do any good. Noah and Blackie were beyond help, but somewhere in this house was the person who had killed them.

He retraced his steps to the entrance to the west wing and walked down the hall to Tip's room. The door was locked but Forsythe banged on it until it opened a crack. The houseman peered into the hall, his eyes widened, and he opened the door all the way. "What in hell?" The brilliant blue eyes wandered from the stains on Forsythe's pajamas to the blood on his mouth. "Are you hurt?"

"Ring up the police. There's been another murder."

The Mexican backed away and the barrister noticed all he was wearing was red boxer shorts. "Jesus! Lucia or Funicelli?"

"Noah Flower."

'Noah . . .'' Tip seized the other man's arm. "Get over here and sit down." He spilled liquor into a glass and offered it. When Forsythe shook his head, he bolted the drink himself. "Where?"

"The courtyard. Make that call *now*."

Tip lifted the receiver. He spoke, waited, and spoke again. He turned to Forsythe. "Be right here. At least Lewis can't blame this on Jacob. Look, Mr. Forsythe, you'd better get cleaned up. Get those pajamas off and wash up." He fished in a drawer. "Here, put these on."

By the time the police arrived, Robert Forsythe was wearing—and not even noticing—jeans and a sweat shirt proclaiming RAISE THE TITANIC!

With the arrival of the police from Great Whitsun, the courtyard brightened. Lights in the roof sprang to life and

147

beamed brightly down on that tropical area. Tip stood in the doorway watching the bustle, but Forsythe remained seated, his back to the glass door. The first officer to reach them was Superintendent Lewis, stepping in from the courtyard. He said harshly, "I understand, Mr. Forsythe, that you found the body of—"

"Get the hell away from me!" Forsythe slowed his voice, spacing his words. "I'll speak with either Inspector Dolan or the chief constable. Not to you."

Lewis didn't argue. As he retreated to the courtyard, Tip muttered, "Nice going."

"If that pompous fool hadn't been trying so hard to please the powerful Mr. Funicelli, Noah might still be alive," Forsythe grated.

It seemed a long time before Inspector Dolan entered the room from the hall. His chin was shadowed with bristles and his face was haggard. Behind him was a constable. "You want to make your statement to me, Mr. Forsythe?"

"Right. Have the rest of the household been checked out?"

"All safe. They've all been rooted out of bed." Dolan smiled faintly. "Velvet gloves are now off. I took the preliminary statements and Mr. Lewis and Sir Cecil are handling the interviews."

"Any results?"

Sinking into another chair, the inspector flipped through the pages of a notebook. "Lucia Funicelli is in the clear. WPC Evans vouched for her." He glanced up. "Do you want this in detail?"

"Please."

"WPC Evans states that she was with Mrs. Lucia Funicelli from noon on. They spent the afternoon and evening in the master suite in the upper west wing. Shortly after six this evening, Mr. Funicelli and his mother came back from Great Whitsun and joined Evans and Lucia in the sitting room of the suite. Mrs. Rosa Funicelli was only there for about half an hour, but Mr. Funicelli stayed with his wife until a few minutes after nine. Dinners on trays were brought up about seven-thirty, and Lucia and Anthony watched television for a time. After he left, WPC Evans and Mrs. Funicelli went to bed. Evans was sleeping on a cot in Mrs. Funicelli's bedroom and swears her charge didn't leave the room until we roused them a short time ago.''

The barrister nodded. "That provides Lucia with an alibi. I understand Anthony was sleeping in a guest room near his mother.''

Dolan flipped more pages. "Correct. Mr. Funicelli says he went directly from his own suite down to the east wing lower. He stopped in to say good night to his mother. Mrs. Rosa Funicelli was preparing to go to bed and noticed her son was looking rather awful, so she insisted on giving him one of her sleeping capsules. As a rule, Mr. Funicelli says he won't touch them, but he did feel he wouldn't sleep well, so he went on to the room that had been prepared for him, took the capsule, and went immediately to bed.''

"And Mama Rosa?''

"Said she also took a capsule and went to bed shortly after she said good night to her son.''

Forsythe cocked his head. "Any signs of those capsules when Mama Rosa and Mr. Funicelli were roused?''

Dolan grinned. "I had the devil's own time getting Mr. Funicelli awake. He was groggy and dazed and said he felt as though he had a giant hangover. Mrs. Rosa Funicelli was in better shape, but then, she takes those things often and probably they don't have the same effect on her as they did on her son.''

Forsythe templed his fingers and gazed down at them. "What did the twins say?''

This time, the inspector didn't consult his notebook. "Much the same story. They stated they had a swim and lunch with you in the courtyard and after that, they went to their studio and spent the afternoon and most of the evening crating their hobby work to have sent back to Vermont. They say they were expecting to go to London tomorrow on the first stage of their trip back to the States. They claim they went to bed between ten and eleven and slept soundly.'' Dolan snapped the book closed and handed it to the constable. "I might better take your statement now, Mr. Delcardo.''

Tip presented rather an odd sight. His hair was standing

149

up around his swarthy face and he'd pulled his mess jacket on over the red boxer shorts. He'd been working on another drink and now he put his glass down and took a deep breath. "I haven't really much to say. No alibi. And it did happen right out there." He waved at the glass door. "Here goes. From about six this evening until after eight, I made up trays and trotted them around to the family's quarters and Mr. Forsythe's room. I left Mr. Forsythe until last and got back down here about half past eight. I did some kitchen chores and decided to leave the trays to collect until morning."

"Yes," Dolan said. "I noticed the trays in the halls."

"Then I checked the lower doors and locked the one leading from the rear of the courtyard—"

"You're certain that door was locked?"

"Positive. Mr. Funicelli is very particular about that door. Claims if anyone got in from the grounds, it might be dangerous for the family. You see, not many of them bother to lock the glass doors leading from the courtyard. Anyway, after I made the rounds, I came back here, read for awhile, had a nightcap, and tumbled into bed. I was dead to the world until Mr. Forsythe banged on the door."

"And you went to bed at what time?"

Tip ran a hand through his untidy hair. "I can't tell you to the minute, but it must have been . . . I'd say shortly before eleven."

"Thank you." Dolan turned to the barrister. "Mr. Forsythe?"

Forsythe made his statement and the constable took it down. When he'd finished, the inspector sighed. "We found no keys on the boy's body. Someone had to have unlocked that door and let him into the courtyard." He looked hopefully at the barrister. "Any ideas?"

"How well did you know Noah Flower?"

"I met him for the first time yesterday. While the super was interviewing Jacob and Mrs. Flower, I asked the lad a few questions. Obviously, he was retarded."

"Noah was an innocent, trusting child. Someone must have enticed him to the courtyard, unlocked that wooden

150

door, and admitted him. The dog may have made a fuss, or the murderer wanted Noah on his knees. Noah may have been a child mentally but physically he was big and powerful. So, the dog was kicked and killed and Noah got down beside it. The murderer drove the knife into the boy's back. Noah crawled away toward the palm, was followed, and . . . Have you any idea how many times the boy was stabbed, Inspector?"

"The medical examiner says four times. One shallow one and three deep ones. Incidently, the butcher knife came from a set they have in the kitchen. Honed very sharp. The handle was wiped clean of prints and—"

Dolan broke off and turned his head. Tip had been perched on the edge of his rumpled bed but now he was on his feet, a hand clapped over his mouth. He ran into the bathroom, leaving the door open. They could hear him vomiting.

The inspector jerked his head toward the open door and the constable shut it. "I don't blame Mr. Delcardo," Dolan said. "This is a sickening business. Anyway, to finish the medical report. The medical examiner estimates time of death shortly after eleven-thirty. Does that square with what you noticed, Mr. Forsythe?"

The barrister nodded. "When I found the body, it was still warm. He must have been stabbed shortly before I went out on the balcony. Possibly I only missed seeing the murderer by a matter of minutes."

Dolan's hand rasped across his chin. "The boy must have cried for help. Why didn't anyone hear him?"

"Soundproofing and double-glazed glass. And probably most people were like me, sound asleep."

The bathroom door opened and Tip stumbled over to the bed. His swarthy face had a greenish tinge. Collapsing on the bed, he rolled over, turning his face to the wall. He muttered, "Could you find somewhere else to talk?"

"Of course." Dolan led the way to the hall. He said to the constable, "You stay down here, Jarvis. Come along, Mr. Forsythe." He stopped in the conversation pit and looked around. The only other person there was another constable, standing near the front door. Dolan called, "I've posted Jarvis in the west wing lower. Did you get the other men posted?"

"Colter's in the upper east wing, sir, and Meade's in the lower east. WPC Evans is still in Mrs. Funicelli's room and Janson's been told to stay in the courtyard."

Inspector Dolan nodded and muttered to the barrister, "Nothing like locking the barn door . . . Okay if we talk in your room?"

"Right." Forsythe led the way up the staircase.

The doors to both the office and den were closed but a murmur of voices could be heard on the balcony. Dolan pointed at the den door. "The chief constable's questioning Mr. Funicelli and his mother in there and the super has the daughter and son in the office."

"How does Superintendent Lewis strike you?"

Dolan's eyes narrowed and he said shortly, "Mr. Lewis is my superior, you know."

"I'm aware of that."

"He's only been at Great Whitsun for a couple of months and this is his first case involving murder." Dolan glanced at the office door and lowered his voice. "He came to us from Birmingham and what I can't figure out is, if he's as good as he thinks he is, what he's doing in a market town like Great Whitsun." The inspector threw discretion to the winds. "Anyway, I've a hunch he won't be with us much longer. Sir Cecil is practically livid."

Behind the door to the east wing, another, younger, constable was lounging. He snapped to attention and the inspector paused to speak to him. Forsythe went on to his own room and, finding it hot and dark, switched on a couple of lamps, shut the glass door, and picked up the duvet from the floor. He turned on the air conditioning and cool air started to hiss into the room. By the time the inspector joined him, the barrister was slumped in an armchair. He gestured the policeman to the other. Dolan glanced around. "Looks like a better-class hotel room. This whole place is weird. Doesn't seem like a home at all."

"We're in agreement on that." Forsythe reached for his

pipe and tobacco pouch but his hand was shaky and tobacco spilled down the borrowed sweat shirt.

"Care for one of these?" Dolan dug out a pack of cigarettes and the barrister took one. Dolan lit both cigarettes and tucked his lighter back into a sagging pocket. "I'll try and make this brief, sir. Can see it's tough on you. But . . . why in hell was that harmless boy killed? Why didn't the murderer go after Mr. Funicelli? WPC Evans was with his wife, but Mr. Funicelli was a sitting duck. Sleeping a drugged sleep and hadn't even bothered to lock his doors."

Forsythe's brow furrowed. "There can be only one reason. Noah Flower presented some kind of danger to the person who shot Fredo Clemenza."

"What kind of danger could a poor dim kid pose?"

"That's what I was trying to figure out while I was waiting for you." The barrister was smoking in quick jerky puffs. "Noah's dog had an uncertain bladder and the boy had to take him out frequently at night. Noah must have seen something, heard something." Ash fell unheeded down Forsythe's sweat shirt. "Yesterday . . . I was talking to the boy and he said something that meant nothing to me at the time."

"What?"

"He said . . . let me think. His exact words were 'Mister, those people do funny things, don't they?' "

"*Funny* things? Like what?"

"I've no idea." Forsythe shrugged. "If I'd thought about it at the time, I might have considered Noah was talking about the officers who took his brother away."

"It could also have been the people in this house." The inspector ground out his cigarette. "Wouldn't Noah have told his mother about the 'funny things'? Wouldn't he have told her if someone had asked him to come to the rear door of the courtyard?"

The barrister considered and then shook his head. "Not necessarily. Remember we're dealing with a child here. Noah had no comprehension about murder or violence. He wouldn't be afraid or—"

"Be quite willing to take candy from strangers?"

"Right. And, like all children, Noah liked a secret. And

153

it could have been concerned with something he wanted to hide from his mother.''

''Such as?''

The barrister tugged at his lower lip. ''What did you say before, inspector? About strangers?''

Dolan cocked his head. ''Kids taking candy from—''

''That's it!'' Forsythe banged a fist on his knee. ''Sweets! Peony! Noah wasn't allowed to even say his sister's name and he missed her. She smuggled him sweets and played games with him. She sent him a card and Jacob tore it up. If Noah was told that a message or a gift had been sent to him from Peony, he'd keep it secret.''

Dolan pulled himself up wearily and tugged down his jacket. ''It looks as though we're dealing with a particularly dirty bastard, Mr. Forsythe. And we'd better get that bastard fast.''

Robert Forsythe raised icy eyes. ''We will, Inspector, I assure you we definitely will.''

CHAPTER FOURTEEN

Long after Dolan left, Forsythe sat huddled in his chair. Finally, he took down his pigskin case, pulled out his flask, and took it into the bathroom. He filled a glass half full, reached for the shower control, and changed his mind. He started to run a hot tub.

Taking a sip of whiskey, he gazed at his reflection in the mirrored wall. Tip's clothes hung on him, making him look like a scarecrow. The jeans were too wide, too short, bagging at the crotch and knees, coming to a stop above his ankles. His face was the color of ashes, dark rings encircled his eyes, dried blood crusted his lower lip, white sand crusted his bare ankles. He stripped off the jeans and sweat shirt, stuck them in a clothes hamper, and went back to the bedroom for corduroy slacks and an Aran sweater the color of Jersey cream.

When the tub was full almost to overflowing, he balanced the glass on the wide edge and eased his weary body into steaming water, which slopped over the edge onto the tiled floor. The hot water was comforting and he raised his knee and massaged it. As he looked at that hand moving over his knee, he saw other hands. Mama Rosa's elegant hand handing a fragile china cup to him, the tanned hand of Hansel on the frame of his doll painting, Funicelli's hand crawling like a hairy spider over his wife's throat and the curve of one white breast, seeking frantically for signs of life, Tip's swarthy hand tenderly touching the photograph of his family, Lucia's chubby hand inching toward a forbidden bread roll.

Forsythe's eyes went from his hand to his knee, from the scars on that knee back to the hand. Little things . . . his forte. Little inconsequential things recurring over and over again, quite unnoticed. Sitting up, he reached for the soap and lathered his chest, thinking furiously. Then he was out of the tub, toweling his lean body, reaching for his clothes.

He drained the glass and hurried to the desk in the bedroom. The digital clock was blinking redly: 7:31. He picked up the phone and dialed. It rang twice and then he heard a familiar voice repeating the number. "Sandy?"

"Robby! About time I heard from you. I understand you're involved with murder again." At the other end, there was a babble of noise and Miss Sanderson said, "One moment, Robby." In the background, there was a crash, a childish squeal, and then her voice, farther away. "Paul, you and Peter get out to the kitchen and sit down. Stay put or you'll be getting porridge instead of waffles." Her voice sounded in Forsythe's ear again. "Honestly, Robby, those boys are enough to try the patience of a saint. Thank God their mother will soon be well enough to take over. After Peter and Paul, even a murder seems rather tame."

He told her grimly, "You wouldn't say that if you'd seen the body I just did."

"Another murder? Blimey!" Her voice rose shrilly. "Tell me about it. Can I help?"

"Calm down, Sandy. I'll fill you in later. Right now, I want a number where Buffy can be reached. Say his—"

"You're in luck. Buffy's here. Came down last evening to see his mother and stayed over. One moment."

Three minutes blinked by on the digital clock before Forsythe heard Buffy's breathless voice. "Aunt Abigail says there's been another murder. Is Anthony—"

"Safe, Buffy. I've a question. Have you ever heard of a physician named Angus Gorinmeister?"

"Not only heard of him but I attended a couple of lectures he's given. A noted man in his field, with a practice in the high-rent district."

"Harley Street?"

"The same. What do you want to know about him?"

Forsythe was doodling on the edge of the sheet he'd used to draw a plan of the Dower House. He'd printed *doctors* and drawn two circles around the word. "Tell me, would I take a sore arm, say a case of bursitis, to Gorinmeister?"

Laughter echoed in the barrister's ear. "Hardly. He happens to be a foremost urologist. In case I've lost you, that means he specializes in urine and the genito-urinary tract."

"You didn't lose me. Another question. Have you ever heard of a doctor called . . . hold on a minute. Pablo . . ." A village, Forsythe thought, but what in hell was the name of that village? Then he had it. "Pablo Quila."

"Sounds Spanish. Where does this doctor practice?"

"Mexico City."

The line hummed and then Buffy Sanderson said hesitantly, "I'm only a medical student. Maybe I could ask around, see if anyone has heard of him. But it's a long shot."

"Extremely long. Never mind, Buffy, the police will be able to move on this. Thanks."

"Have I been of any help?"

"You've no idea of how much."

"Mr. Forsythe—"

"Robert."

"Sorry, I forgot. Robert, please look after Anthony."

"I'm going to do just that."

There was a sound in the background and the boy said hastily, "Hang on. Aunt Abigail wants to talk to—"

"No time. Tell Sandy I'll satisfy her curiosity later."

The barrister hung up, stared down at his doodling, and then reached for the bell. When Tip put in an appearance, he was wearing a fresh mess jacket and had plastered down his hair, but his skin was still muddy. "If

157

you're thinking of food," he said, "I'm afraid you'll have to forage for it in the kitchen. Sorry, but my stomach is churning and I—"

"Food is the furthest thing from my mind. Are Sir Cecil and Inspector Dolan still here?"

"Having a conference on the balcony." Tip's face brightened. "That storm trooper Lewis has gone back to Great Whitsun. I've a hunch he's in disgrace."

"And he should be." Forsythe got up and moved toward the hall door. "Come along, Tip."

The houseman eyed him warily. "What's up, Mr. Forsythe?"

Forsythe managed a faint smile. "Education time. I'm giving you a chance to watch another Clarence Darrow at work."

Both the chief constable and the inspector were leaning against the railing of the balcony. Sir Cecil looked as though he needed that railing as a support. He turned tired sad eyes toward the barrister. "We were both right about Jacob Flower," he said. "But it's cold comfort. I've had to tell Mrs. Flower about Noah—"

"I know." Forsythe touched Sir Cecil's sleeve. "I think we'd better talk and I want Tip with us. Inspector, would you have your constable down there bring up that black trench coat from the closet near the front door?"

Dolan looked puzzled but called down to the constable. When the man trotted up the stairs, the inspector took the coat and handed it to Forsythe. Forsythe fished in the pockets and pulled out a crisp handkerchief, two ticket stubs, and a ball-point pen. He smiled, replaced them, and carried the coat into Funicelli's den. The four men found chairs and Forsythe took a look around the room. Butter-colored leather chairs and a matching sofa, two walls lined with mystery books, a table centered with a wedding photograph. Lucia was wearing a fussy white gown and a halo of orange blossoms adorned her long hair. At her side, a radiantly proud Anthony Funicelli beamed. Mama Rosa stood regally and gracefully at her son's side and beside the bride was an enormously fat woman with a strong facial resemblance to Lucia.

The chief constable cleared his throat. "Ah," he prompted.

Forsythe turned to the inspector. "Do you have that list I gave you yesterday?"

"Right here." Dolan took a cream-colored sheet from his breast pocket.

"Read what I wrote about the Funicelli twins."

"Hansel and Gretchen Funicelli," Dolan read aloud. "Impossible to think of these two separately. They—"

"The last line."

"Could this whole thing be a monstrous hoax?"

Sir Cecil's thin frame tensed. "Are you saying that the twins sent those letters as a joke, Mr. Forsythe?"

"No. Gretchen and her brother aren't involved in this. They, like Tip and I, were merely spectators at a particularly deadly game. Gentlemen, I don't intend to draw this out. Anthony Funicelli shot his cousin to death and . . . and he butchered Noah Flower."

"Impossible!" Sir Cecil shook his head. "He and his wife were the targets of the murderer. Anthony is half out of his mind for fear that Lucia will be harmed."

"Lucia is not, and never has been, in any danger. Anthony Funicelli happens to be a most accomplished actor."

"This is a serious charge, sir," Dolan said. "Do you want Mr. Funicelli present?"

"I don't wish to see Mr. Funicelli now or ever."

Sir Cecil moved restlessly. "Have you proof to support this allegation?"

"Leads. The proof will be up to you."

"Very well. Continue, Mr. Forsythe."

"Please bear with me. A short time ago, while I was in my bath, I was rubbing a knee that was injured years ago and I had a number of thoughts. I was thinking it would be necessary to consult my physician about a possible operation. My next thought was about this case. So many doctors seemed to be involved. First there was Buford Sanderson, who is a medical student, and he was the one who persuaded me to come to the Dower House. Then there was mention of Dr. Fish, Lucia's obstetrician. I heard of two doctors who Funicelli, who doesn't care for doctors, had consulted. One was Angus Gorinmeister who has a practice on Harley Street, another was Pablo Quila—''

''How do you know that name?'' Tip blurted.

''You told me. Not directly, but you said the reason you liked the Mexican doctor was that his first name is your father's, his surname the name of your village.'' The barrister templed his fingers. ''Shortly before Funicelli's second marriage, he went to Mexico City to have a famous goldsmith make a wedding ring and a crucifix for his future bride. While there, he was supposed to have been hospitalized with what is popularly known as common diarrhea. Then, during his wife's early pregnancy, Funicelli again sought help from Mr. Gorinmeister. Funicelli explained he'd had bursitis.''

''I'm afraid,'' the baronet confessed, ''that I fail to follow you.''

''You will shortly, Sir Cecil.'' Forsythe waved at the houseman. ''I must make one point clear. Anthony Funicelli not only has complete control over Tip, here, but Tip's family's welfare depends on his keeping silent. But . . . the time has come to break that silence. Tip, tell us exactly what you learned when you went to Mexico City to take your employer home.''

''My family, Mr. Forsythe!''

''I give my word that your family will be safe.''

The brilliant blue eyes flared. ''Then you're damned right I'll talk! Maybe I could see him killing Clemenza, but that poor pathetic kid—'' He broke off and then said slowly, ''Mr. Funicelli was hospitalized because he'd had a vasectomy and there were complications. That's why he called Dr. Quila a bungling quack.''

The baronet rubbed at his jutting nose. ''But his wife is *pregnant*.''

''And that was the motive for murder,'' Forsythe said.

160

"Consider Funicelli's position. His family is Catholic, and, while he doesn't pretend to be religious, his mother is devout and his future wife was, too. Funicelli has never concealed his distaste for children. He had twins by his first wife, Ilse, and detests Hansel and Gretchen. Here he was about to marry a young and nubile girl who not only is a devout Catholic but wants a large family. What was the man to do?"

Dolan grinned. "Find a young and nubile girl who wasn't a Catholic."

"But Funicelli had been struck by what he calls the 'thunderbolt.' Lucia was the only woman he wanted and he was determined to have her. To avoid having children, he slipped quietly off to Mexico City and Dr. Quila."

Forsythe looked from one officer's intent face to the other. "Imagine Funicelli's shock when he found Lucia was pregnant. I suppose his first thought was that the 'bungling quack' had failed to make him sterile. He went to Mr. Gorinmeister, not for bursitis, because the man is a noted urologist, but for a sperm count. I'm convinced that Funicelli was assured he was sterile and couldn't have fathered a child."

"The light finally dawns," Dolan said. "Mr. Funicelli decided that his cousin, Fredo Clemenza, was that child's father."

"Exactly. And he had good reason for that. I understand that Clemenza had a history of seducing, at times forcibly, a number of girls. Shortly before this, Funicelli had had to fish his cousin out of another mess with a young—"

"Peony Flower!" Sir Cecil banged a fist on the arm of his chair. "At that time, Mrs. Flower came to me and accused Anthony of having raped her daughter. I took it rather lightly, I fear. I thought Peony, who gave signs of being rather wild, had had an affair with a village lad and was trying to put the blame on Anthony." He looked bewildered. "I can understand why Anthony would be outraged, but to kill his cousin . . ."

"You don't understand Sicilians, Sir Cecil." Tip flashed

his white grin. "Mr. Funicelli's pure young bride had been dishonored. His instinct would be for blood."

Dolan cocked his head. "Do you think Mr. Funicelli confronted his wife? Forced her to give him Clemenza's name?"

The questions had been directed at Forsythe, but it was the Mexican who answered. "That is the last thing my master would do. In all the years I've served him, I've only seen two genuine emotions displayed by Mr. Funicelli. He loves his mother and is also deathly afraid of her disapproval, and he literally worships his wife. Considers her a saint. I imagine he decided his cousin had raped Lucia and the girl was too modest and too ashamed to confess. Anyway, to question his wife would bring the matter of his vasectomy to light. If his mother ever found out about that, she's quite capable of disowning her son." Tip shrugged. "The master also doesn't know his wife very well. Lucia Funicelli is a hot-blooded girl and her husband was frequently away from home. I don't think Fredo had to resort to force. Lucia may have found an affair with her husband's cousin a pleasant way to wile away the time."

Forsythe had been sitting back, lighting another of Dolan's cigarettes. Now he said, "I agree with Tip's conclusions. It's also possible that Lucia, who knows nothing about the vasectomy, believes her husband *is* the father of this baby. Funicelli must have felt quite safe in plotting his revenge. The only one who knew about the vasectomy was Tip, and Funicelli, regardless of what happened, could blackmail the houseman into keeping quiet."

The baronet shook his head. "I disagree with that conclusion, Mr. Forsythe. It appears to me that it would be Mr. Delcardo who would be able to blackmail his employer."

Again the Mexican answered. "You don't really know Anthony Funicelli, sir. He moves with lightning speed, like a—"

"Snake?" Forsythe suggested.

Tip jerked his head in agreement. "He made it quite clear it would only take one phone call and my family would either be in jail or on their way back to Mexico. I couldn't expose him."

"To continue," Forsythe said, "Rosa Funicelli came from Chicago to look after Lucia, and shortly afterward, Hansel and Gretchen arrived at the Dower House. Funicelli made careful plans to murder his cousin and ensure no suspicion would be cast on him. He got Buford Sanderson to this house, not because of fondness for the boy, but to find an excuse for having me on the scene when—"

"Pardon me," Sir Cecil said politely. "I should think you'd be the last person Anthony would want around if he was planning a crime."

"Funicelli overestimated himself and underestimated me. I was to be an impartial witness, one to swear that Funicelli was in fear of his life. A witness to testify to those letters. He had already picked Jacob Flower to be the scapegoat and believed I'd immediately concentrate on him.

"Funicelli wrote the series of threatening letters and stuck the letterheads in Jacob's old jacket in the greenhouse. He mailed the letters to himself at spaced intervals. One was to coincide with Buffy's arrival, one with mine. Shortly after I arrived, he put the plan into operation. Again I was to testify, this time that Funicelli, not Clemenza, was the target. The night of Clemenza's death, his cousin set the scene. They played backgammon and Funicelli let Fredo win. Fredo drank a great deal of bourbon and Funicelli arranged that I would discover the body. Then he pretended to go for a walk."

"He didn't walk far, did he?" Dolan asked.

"All Funicelli did was wait by one of the windows of the manor until I went up into the east wing. Then he trotted around the house, up the metal steps, unlocked a fire exit, and came in on the balcony. He forced the drawer on his desk and took the revolver. Funicelli then called down to his cousin and probably told Fredo that he'd remembered an important paper in his briefcase that he must look over immediately." Forsythe butted his cigarette and continued. "Fredo was only too happy to do a service for his cousin. He picked up the briefcase—"

"The *lift*," Dolan said. "Mr. Clemenza was never known to have used that lift."

"To bear out Funicelli's story, it was essential his cousin use the lift. Clemenza was elated by his victory in their game, he was befuddled with alcohol, he yearned to please his cousin." Forsythe gazed at the wedding photograph, at the groom's smiling face. "I can almost see, almost hear, what happened. Funicelli, standing against the railing, the revolver behind his back, joked with Clemenza. He probably called down something like 'Don't be a stick in the mud, Fredo. Mama Rosa isn't around. Try the lift.' " The barrister rubbed his eyes. "We'll never know exactly what was said, but we do know Funicelli persuaded Fredo to get on that lift. When Fredo leaned down to pick up the brief-case—"

"Bang!" Tip cried.

Sir Cecil darted a disapproving look at the Mexican. "And then Anthony retraced his steps, waited outside until the lights went on in the balcony, and then came in as though returning from his walk."

Forsythe nodded. "With the exception of one detail, you're correct. Funicelli had a detour to make. He had to bury something."

The inspector's brow wrinkled. "What?"

"A pair of black leather gloves. The right glove with traces of nitrate on the palm of it. Damning evidence against Anthony Funicelli."

The baronet confessed, "Again, I fail to follow your reasoning, Mr. Forsythe."

"Hands," Forsythe muttered. "That was the other thought I had in the tub. My mind was drifting and I was picturing hands, all the hands of the people in this house. I saw Funicelli's hairy hands, the night of his cousin's murder, on his wife's sleeping body, pretending to search for signs of life. Then, my mind flashed back to the earlier part of that evening.

"You see, I have a trained memory. Not as good as my secretary's, because Sandy's mind is close to photographic, but mine is much better than most people's. Again I saw Funicelli in the conversation pit, putting on a black trench

164

coat, pulling on black leather gloves. Then I remembered him reentering the house, calling up to his cousin, racing up the stairs. From that point on, I was with him every moment until you arrived. When Funicelli got to his wife's room with me, I noticed his hands were bare, yet he hadn't taken off any gloves when he came into the house. So, the question is, where are those gloves?''

Dolan said abruptly, ''He could have taken them off outside, jammed them in his pockets.'' He glanced at the black trench coat thrown over the leather sofa. ''Ah!''

Forsythe rubbed his brow. ''Sir Cecil, Funicelli took that coat off in the conversation pit, shortly after he phoned you. He threw it across a chair.'' He turned his head. ''Tip, has he worn that coat since?''

''No. When I tidied up the conversation pit the following morning, the coat was on a chair and I hung it in the closet. I swear that there were no gloves in the pockets at that time. I would have noticed the bulges. Since then . . .'' Tip frowned. ''Mr. Funicelli has only left the house once. Yesterday, when he and his mother went to Great Whitsun. But he was wearing his vicuña coat and light brown gloves.''

'' 'Those people do funny things,' '' Inspector Dolan quoted.

''One did,'' Forsythe agreed. ''Noah saw the man from the Dower House, the one he was much in awe of, doing very funny things. The boy was walking his dog and saw that man looking in a window, running around to the fire escape, digging a hole at the edge of the knot garden—''

''Why the knot garden?''

''The kitchen garden wasn't spaded over until yesterday morning. Noah was doing it, but the previous day he'd been working at the knot garden. The only soft earth was right there, at the edges of it. Funicelli was pressed for time, so he buried the gloves there and Noah saw him.'' Forsythe sighed heavily. ''Noah was a child, curious as small children always are. After Funicelli went back into the house, the boy dug those gloves up and kept them. You see, his dog liked to chew at leather. I saw Blackie gnawing at Noah's leather cap.''

The baronet straightened his storklike frame. "Do you think Anthony spotted Noah and the dog that night?"

The barrister shook his head. "No. Noah was nervous of the man from the Dower House. I should imagine that Noah kept well back and Funicelli had no idea he was there. Funicelli must have felt quite safe at that point. He'd revenged his wife's honor, Fredo was dead, and Jacob Flower was going to be charged with Fredo's murder. Again, Funicelli received a shock. He found there had been a witness and that witness had the damning gloves."

"But how?" Sir Cecil asked. "The only time he left this house he was with his mother."

"The morning after the murder, when I was heading down to the gate house to question Mrs. Flower, Mama Rosa and Funicelli came out to drive to Great Whitsun. Funicelli told his mother to wait by the front door and he circled around to the rear to get the car from the garage. I'd reached the gate house, a fair walk from the front of the house and I wasn't walking quickly, before their car passed me. Funicelli had plenty of time for a conversation with Noah."

Dolan said, "And the boy mentioned the gloves?"

"He probably blurted it out, Inspector. Possibly told Funicelli he had hidden them and could he keep them for toys for his dog. Funicelli thought fast, made an appointment for the boy to go to the rear door of the courtyard that night and return the gloves. I should imagine Funicelli was kind and jovial with the boy. And then he baited the trap and I know exactly how he did it. Noah missed his sister. Peony played games with him and smuggled him sweets. That's how Funicelli got Noah to keep it a secret from his mother. Either he told the boy he had a message from his sister or that she'd sent some sweets."

"And we know the rest," the baronet said grimly. "I still can't see why the boy had to die. Surely Anthony could simply have taken the gloves, given the lad some sweets, and sent him home. Did Anthony panic?"

"The master never panics," Tip said flatly.

"But no one would have listened to Noah," the chief constable protested.

"*I* would have." Forsythe's mouth hardened. "Funicelli knew I didn't believe that Jacob Flower was guilty and he realized he'd made a mistake bringing me in on it. He knew I'd go on digging and I'd pay attention to Noah. Indirectly, I'm responsible for the boy's death."

Dolan had been making notes. He glanced up at the chief constable. "We have two good leads, sir. Mr. Gorinmeister and Dr. Quila. They won't be hard to check out. But that's hardly enough evidence to warrant an arrest."

The baronet pointed his jutting nose at the inspector. "Where is Anthony now?"

"He wanted to go to the upper west wing to be with his wife. I had Lauden escort him there and Evans is still with Mrs. Funicelli. I told Lauden to stay with them, too."

"And there are men posted in the other wings, the courtyard, the manor?"

"Of course, sir."

"There was, of course, no possibility of the murderer of Noah Flower committing that . . . that butchery without getting blood on his clothes?"

Forsythe had already thought of this but he sat back watching, with much amusement, the man he'd once thought so vague and hesitant.

"A thorough search has been conducted for bloodstained clothes, sir. We did find striped pajamas with stains in the laundry hamper in Mr. Delcardo's bathroom, but they belong to Mr. Forsythe." Dolan glanced at the barrister and he nodded. "Nothing else has been found."

"And your search included the guest room in the lower east wing where Anthony Funicelli so conveniently spent the night?"

"No, sir. At that point we thought Mr. Funicelli was the target of the murderer. . . . My God!" Dolan leaped up and bolted from the room.

Forsythe was smiling widely. "Do you still think, Sir Cecil, that you're too old for this job?"

The baronet beamed back. "As Holmes would say, elementary, my dear Watson. Obviously, Anthony has had no chance to get rid of those clothes. You raised the alarm too quickly. Ergo . . . they're tucked away somewhere in that room."

"And the gloves!" Tip said gleefully.

"Exactly. A nice tight case against Anthony Funicelli. I wish," Sir Cecil said mildly, "I could watch him hang, but I've no doubt he'll be receiving a long sentence in an English prison." He transferred the smile to Tip. "Mr. Delcardo, you've been of inestimable assistance to us. Mr. Forsythe, I'm certain you're eager to leave. No doubt you'll be needed later, but then, ah, we know where to find you."

"There's nothing that would please me more, sir." Forsythe pulled himself to his feet. "Tip, could you drive me to the station?"

The Mexican consulted his watch. "The next train isn't until late afternoon."

"No problem." Sir Cecil waved a hand. "I'll put my car and chauffeur at your disposal, Mr. Forsythe. Henty is like me, getting a bit long in the tooth, but he's an excellent driver."

"You sit down, Mr. Forsythe," Tip said. "I'll get your case packed."

Forsythe accepted both offers. He was eager to get away from this house. In a remarkably short time, the ancient chauffeur had tucked him into the back of Sir Cecil's car and stowed his luggage into the trunk and the venerable Rolls was smoothly heading toward London. The car might have been old but she was a beauty. Next to Forsythe in the rear seat, hyacinth, pink and purple, wafted fragrance from crystal bud vases.

By the time they rolled through Great Whitsun, Forsythe, cradled on soft upholstery and lulled by warm air scented with hyacinth and lemon oil, was sound asleep.

He didn't dream of the Dower House or bloodstained bodies. Instead, for a time, he was with Jennifer Dorland on the beach at Acapulco. The sun beamed down on them and Jennifer's long hair drifted across his face. Contentedly, he inhaled the fragrance, a faint odor of honey, that was Jennifer's alone.

CHAPTER FIFTEEN

The cold, wet, miserable spring weather lasted well into June, but July and August proceeded to break every record for high temperatures. Robert Forsythe found the hot weather to his liking. His bad leg was always less painful in the heat and so he postponed or, as Miss Sanderson caustically remarked, chickened out on the leg operation he'd been considering.

The final day of August found him in the kitchen of his flat, bending over a simmering pot. Miss Sanderson, looking most fetching in apple green linen, was leaning against the sink. Her narrow waist was cinched by an emerald green belt and a similar color flashed from the antique emerald pendant Forsythe had given her the previous Christmas.

"You continually surprise me, Robby," she said. "I had no idea your cooking ability ran to anything but tossing salads and burning chops."

"You of little faith. I thought I'd try a stew. They don't seem that difficult."

"They aren't. Trick is in seasoning them properly. Here, let an expert taste that mulligan." Spooning up some liquid, she blew on it and took a cautious sip. "Needs more salt and some oregano. And for a proper stew—" She opened the door of the fridge. "Just as I thought. Leftovers. The cardinal rule with mulligans is to get rid of all odds and ends. What do we have here? Two boiled potatoes, some wizened peas, a dry chunk of Cheddar pushed to the back of a shelf. Stand aside, Robby.''

''You're going to ruin it! The cooking book says—''

''Nonsense. Next rule is throw out the cooking book and go by taste.'' Brushing him aside, she sliced potatoes into the pot, dumped in the peas, crumbled cheese, and sprinkled herbs. ''Doesn't Mrs. Tupper look after your meals?''

''Mrs. Tupper is spending a couple of weeks with a niece in Brighton. I got tired of restaurant food and decided to cook my dinner.''

''And decided to make stew on one of the hottest days this summer.'' Miss Sanderson briskly stirred. ''If it had been December, I suppose you'd have decided on ice-cold vichyssoise. Here, have a taste.''

Forsythe took a sip from the wooden spoon she was extending. ''Delicious! You are an expert.''

''I'm an expert at more than mulligans. Where in hell did you get that outfit? And, more importantly, why?''

Forsythe adjusted his butcher's apron over new well-fitting jeans and a spanking white T-shirt. ''Sandy, you're the one who is always urging me to come up-to-date.''

''Well . . .'' Her pale blue eyes slid down his lean frame. ''I suppose it does no harm to wear them around the flat.''

''Actually, I was considering wearing them in chambers.''

''Blimey! You'll send young Peters into another fit of nerves and give Mrs. Sutter cardiac arrest. Face it, Robby. You're not the type for jeans.''

He sighed. ''So Tip Delcardo told me. By the way, he should be here shortly. Are you anxious to meet him?''

''Can hardly wait.'' She looked searchingly up at him. ''Are you actually going through with this?''

''Put your money on it.''

''Injured vanity?''

''Partly. No one really enjoys an ego-bashing.''

''What's the other part?''

Forsythe's mouth opened, but the door bell chimed. He made a move, but his secretary said, ''Better peel off that apron. I'll introduce myself and practice some Spanish on him. Might as well make use of all those lessons."

She left the kitchen door ajar and as Forsythe took off his apron, turned down the heat under the pot, and stuck a lid on the stew, he could hear the murmur of voices from the hall. When he reached the living room, Tip was wandering along the wall of books, his hands clasped behind him. Forsythe called a greeting, and without turning, Tip said, "I like your flat, Mr. Forsythe. Nice old building, big rooms with high ceilings, lots of books and antique furnishings . . . one of these days I'm going to have a home like this."

"Glad you approve, Tip."

The Mexican swung around. His eyes widened when he saw his host's clothes, but he made no comment on them. He said, "I approve of your secretary, too. Speaks quite fluent Spanish."

Miss Sanderson smiled. "Thanks heaps, Mr. Delcardo—"

"Could you make that Tip?"

"I prefer Mr. Delcardo. I was going to mention that you may find a home like Robby's, but you'll never find a secretary like me."

Forsythe grinned. "That's true, Sandy. You're not only unique but amazingly modest. Tip, you're looking most prosperous."

The younger man glanced down at his casual but expensive clothes and passed a complacent hand over nicely styled hair. "Courtesy of Mama Rosa. She's majoring in good deeds, hoping to atone for her son's sins. She started with me. Handed me a check large enough to see me through law school and also to keep me in a style I have every intention of getting used to." Tip wandered over to the bay window. It was open and a warm breeze billowed the curtains and stirred the petals of a mass of white freesia. Sunlight bronzed his rugged profile.

Forsythe eyed that profile. "Did Rosa Funicelli's largess extend to the rest of your family?"

"The Delcardos are now American citizens in good standing and have recently opened a restaurant in San Francisco."

172

Miss Sanderson smoothed gray waves back from her face. "Mexican food? Tacos and enchiladas and—"

"More like Italian. It's kind of a pizzeria. Mother's a fantastic cook."

"I'm sure it will be a success," Miss Sanderson told him. "How would you like a Mexican drink, Mr. Delcardo? Perhaps a margarita?"

He turned to face her. "Sounds good. Do you want me to make it?"

"I'll cope," she told him, and exited the room.

Tip looked after her. "Marvelous lady, but why won't she call me Tip?"

Because, the barrister thought silently, Sandy would never be foolish enough to give a pet name to a chicken she was planning on killing for dinner. Aloud, he said, "Sandy doesn't believe in instant informality. Tell me, how are the Flowers?"

"Jacob and his dour mother are now living in a cottage on Sir Cecil's estate. Mrs. Flower is working as housekeeper-cook and Jacob is gardener." Tip adjusted the collar of his silk shirt and Forsythe noticed it was close to the color of the man's eyes. "Mama Rosa tried to atone to them, too, but Mrs. Flower told her they would accept nothing from a member of the family that had ruined her daughter and killed her son—" Tip broke off and accepted a goblet from the secretary.

She handed her employer a drink and took a sip of her own. "I was eavesdropping, Mr. Delcardo. What did Mrs. Funicelli offer the Flowers?"

"A deed to the gate house and jobs as caretakers." He took a taste and then raised his glass to Miss Sanderson. "My compliments. This is great.

"When the Flowers turned Mama Rosa down cold, I was stuck with looking after the Dower House, which is why I'm still in England. Shortly after the master was arrested, Mama Rosa sent Lucia to Chicago in the care of the twins. Hansel and Gretchen have really rallied around. They even offered to raise Lucia's child when it's born, but Mama Rosa won't consider that. She claims the baby may not be her grandchild

173

but it will be her great-nephew. She also said that although Fredo Clemenza wasn't any good, his mother was a Funicelli.'' Tip flashed his white grin. "Which makes the baby the heir to the Funicelli empire.''

"So you've been living at the Dower House," Forsythe said.

"Looking after the place and closing it down. Mama Rosa refused to stay on in the house. As soon as Lucia and the twins left, she took an apartment in Great Whitsun and stayed there until after her son's trial. Then she headed back to Chicago.''

"What is Mama Rosa's attitude toward her son?''

"About what you could expect from a Sicilian lady. She arranged legal counsel for her son and hung around until he was sentenced. Then she washed her hands of him. I'm inclined to think Funicelli's vasectomy affronted her more than the murders he committed.'' Tip drained his glass and sat down on a chair near the barrister. "She could hardly wait to get back to the States to witness the birth of the new heir.''

Setting down her own empty goblet, Miss Sanderson glanced at Forsythe's. His drink was on the table at his elbow but he hadn't touched it. Sandy's cool eyes moved to the Mexican. "When is Lucia's baby due?''

"The end of next month.'' Tip stretched his stocky frame. "By that time, I should be back in the States, too, and perhaps starting law school. Watch out, world, another Clarence Darrow is on the way!''

Miss Sanderson arched her brows. "*Your* fascination with the law fascinates *me*, Mr. Delcardo. Are you an idealist?''

"Translated, I suppose that means do I intend to put my services at the disposal of the poor downtrodden masses.'' He threw back his head and laughed. "No way, José. Lawyers are generally fat cats and money is my goal. I've had quite enough of being a peon and waiting on other people. I must admit I find the Flower family puzzling. They could have made a nice thing out of Mama Rosa's guilty conscience. If they'd played it right, they—''

"Did it ever occur to you," Forsythe asked sharply, "that the Flowers have ethics?''

174

"Ethics don't buy designer clothes."

Forsythe templed his fingers. "Odd how this whole affair has worked out to your advantage."

The Mexican answered in Spanish and winked at Miss Sanderson. She said crisply, "Robby, Mr. Delcardo just stated that fate has found fit to smile on him and his family."

"With a great big nudge from our wily Mexican, Sandy. Tip, you remember young Davy Crockett and his water pistol?" The younger man nodded and Forsythe said, "As the lad might say, I feel as though I've been hornswoggled by a sidewinder."

"And as Sir Cecil Safrone might say, Mr. Forsythe, I, ah, fail to follow you." Tip's bright eyes fastened on the barrister. "I may be lacking in ethics, but there's nothing wrong with my instincts. When Miss Sanderson phoned and invited me here, I figured we were going to have a few drinks, a few laughs, and a friendly chat. But neither you nor your secretary are friendly. In fact, I sense you're downright hostile."

Miss Sanderson said coldly, "You're instincts are dead on, pardner."

"Here's a tip for Tip," Forsythe said. "I wouldn't count on being another Darrow. You're going to be too busy running and hiding."

"Busy doing *what*?"

"Running and hiding."

Tip sat up and stared from the barrister to his secretary. "You certainly didn't mince words when you exposed Funicelli. If you've something to say about me, spit it out!"

Miss Sanderson said lazily, "Mr. Delcardo, you have beautiful eyes. I've been admiring them. Never have I seen that particular color before. Would you say they're turquoise or closer to sapphire? Or a mixture of both?"

"You're *both* nuts!"

"Perfectly sane," Forsythe drawled. "And about to prove it. I'll admit you had me hoodwinked, but after I told the whole sordid story to Sandy, she started to ask questions. Then the light broke. As you kept reiterating, the Funicellis are Sicilians. But you, Tip, are positively Machiavellian."

"Okay, take your time." Tip settled back comfortably and grinned. "What questions did you ask, Miss Sanderson?"

Holding up a hand, she ticked points off thin fingers. "Why, from the moment you met Robby at the station, were you so candid about Anthony Funicelli and his family? I questioned my nephew and Buffy tells me that with him you simply acted like a meek respectful servant and yet—"

"With Mr. Forsythe, I was chummy and informative. Miss Sanderson, I told your boss why. I liked him and he's a lawyer."

"Weak, Mr. Delcardo. At that time you had no idea what Robby was really like. He could very well have told Funicelli that he had a manservant babbling like a brook about his family. It was a dangerous gamble but the stakes were high and you had to take the chance." Miss Sanderson lit a cigarette and blew a smoke ring. "Then I pointed out to Robby that you'd been most busy giving him winks, feeding him tidbits of information, pointing his nose right at Anthony Funicelli. An example was giving Robby the name of the doctor in Mexico City. An amazing performance from a man whose family's safety depended on absolute silence."

"So I talk a lot." Tip shrugged and turned to the barrister. "Are you trying to say that Funicelli did *not* kill his cousin and that poor kid?"

"Funicelli pulled the trigger and used the knife, yes. But the man responsible for both murders happens to be Felipe Manuel Jesus Delcardo. My wily friend, you created a murderer."

"Ever heard about the law against slander, Mr. Forsythe?"

"This isn't slander. This is the truth."

"Tell on, barrister."

"As you told me, you were 'itchy' to get away from Funicelli. You were more than itchy, you were desperate. I think you got your idea for your own monstrous hoax from two sources. You'd heard the twins' story about their mother's death. I have no doubt that Anthony Funicelli was responsible for Ilse's death and that he used his knowledge of his first wife's character to goad her into getting on that killer

176

horse. Your second idea came from Peony Flower's pregnancy by Fredo Clemenza. You decided to use your master's character against him. Your reasoning was this: If Lucia also became pregnant, Anthony would react with cunning violence. He would immediately conclude that his cousin had forcefully seduced his saintly young wife and—''

"With good reason. Fredo certainly had a yen for young girls."

"Fredo also had a few ethics. As Gretchen told me, during all the years he looked after the twins, he never made a move toward her. You see, Gretchen was family. If Fredo wouldn't touch Anthony's daughter, he certainly wouldn't lay a finger on Anthony's wife."

The Mexican flashed his white grin again. "By George, an immaculate conception!"

Forsythe ignored this remark. "During Anthony's frequent absences, there was another man in the Dower House, a much younger man, a much better-looking man than Fredo Clemenza. A man out to get rid of Funicelli—''

"You think the master's wife would stoop to an affair with a lowly peasant?"

"The master's wife was straight from a tiny village in Sicily. Lucia's a peasant, too, and, as you said, hot-blooded. She also would never betray you to her husband. That code of *omerta* you kept mentioning. And all Lucia was doing was seeking pleasure, sating an appetite similar to the one she has for food. But you, Tip, were *intent* on getting her pregnant. You knew Funicelli would plot Sicilian revenge against his cousin and that's exactly what he did. You used *me* to expose Funicelli, and you knew his mother, an honorable woman, would do the right thing by you and your family."

The Mexican was laughing. "And I won the game, didn't I? No point in denying your reasoning, counselor; it's bang on. The law can't touch me. So far as I know, bedding a lusty, willing wench isn't grounds for legal action."

"True." Forsythe got up and wandered over to the window, touching the petals of the freesia. Sunlight washed over the flowers, sending strong bursts of perfume through the

177

room. He took a deep breath. "Would you say Mama Rosa is an intelligent woman?"

"Smart as a whip. And vindictive as they come. But Mama Rosa will never know I set her son up unless—" Tip was on his feet. "Are you going to tell her?"

"I doubt that will be necessary. In about a month, I think Mama Rosa will be figuring that out all by herself."

The Mexican brushed his hand over his eyes and Miss Sanderson said complacently, "That's right. Those beautiful eyes. As you once told Robby, regardless of the color of a mate's eyes, the children always have the blue Delcardo eyes. Blimey, but did you outsmart yourself!"

Tip looked stunned and Forsythe said evenly, "How do you think Mama Rosa is going to react when she looks down at Lucia's baby and sees those blue eyes of yours staring back?"

"She'll know," Tip whispered. "She'll know I set her son up and . . . Oh God! That woman is capable of anything. Even sending a hit man after me." He held out an imploring hand. "My *family*."

"Don't worry about your family. Mama Rosa's a fair woman. They'll be safe. You're the one she'll go after."

"Look," Tip blurted, "I never dreamed anything would happen to Noah Flower. When he was killed, I felt *terrible*."

"I know that, Tip. I was there and saw your reaction to the boy's death." Forsythe's words fell like chips of ice in the warm room. "But you started Funicelli on his killing rampage and I hold you responsible for Noah Flower's death. Better start running; it won't be long before someone's on your trail."

Tip shivered. He said slowly, "There's an old saying in my country that the wise man knows when to vanish."

"We have an old saying, too. Vengeance has a long arm and the hand is bloody."

Tip headed toward the archway leading to the hall. Then he stopped and swung around. "I'm losing my head. Look, genetics don't always run true. Dark brown eyes are as much a characteristic of the Funicelli family as blue eyes are of mine. Consider the twins. They have their mother's flaxen

178

hair and white skin and the dark Funicelli eyes. Lucia's child may have brown eyes. I may still be in the clear.''

"You're considering a miracle may save you.'' Forsythe tugged at his lower lip. Then he said decisively, "If that miracle does occur, I assure you you're still not in the clear. I've every intention of giving justice a nudge.''

"You'd rat on me to Mama Rosa?''

"I would.''

"Do you think she'd believe you?''

Forsythe's lips twitched in a faint smile. "Do *you* think she would?''

"You—'' The Mexican lunged into the hall. He shouted a few Spanish words and then the front door crashed closed behind him.

Forsythe returned to his chair and his secretary winced. "Would you like a translation on that last remark?''

"Not necessary. But you could empty this margarita down the sink and pour me a glass of whiskey.''

When she handed him the squat glass, she asked, "Do you actually intend to tell Rosa Funicelli who maneuvered her son into prison by impregnating his wife?''

"If necessary, yes.''

"You said it wasn't only because of that bashing your ego took and you're not spiteful.'' She gave him a long level look. "Why?''

"Gethsemane.'' Robert Forsythe looked off into space. "Because of a child named Noah, Sandy, and a little dog he called Blackie.''

ABOUT THE AUTHOR

E. X. Giroux has written six earlier novels about her delight-ful amateur sleuths, barrister Robert Forsythe and his sec-retary Abigail. The most recent was *A Death for a Dreamer*. She lives in Fraser Glen, British Columbia, not far from Vancouver.